A BOUNTY OF STARS

A Sci-fi Romance

Constellation Contracts
Book 1

LAUREN WINTHER

A Bounty of Stars by Lauren Winther

laurenwinther.com

Copyright © 2022 Lauren Winther

Cover by Lauren Winther

Editing by Kendra Nuttall

ISBN: 979-8-9866640-1-9 (Print)

*For all my wonderful friends who
support my crazy ideas.*

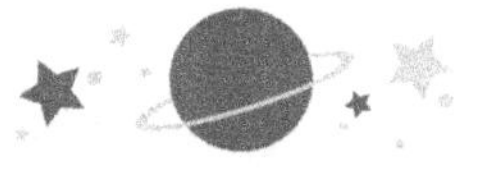

Author's Note

This book contains themes for older audiences including alien abduction, violence, death, religious trauma, steamy romance scenes (consensual) and mentions of prostitution.

ONE

Star System #30003 (AKA, Earth's Star System)

VALERIE

Ten in the evening was arguably not the best time for coffee. As neither a college student, nor someone working graves, I had no business being here this late. The smell of fresh coffee filled my nose as I placed my order—an americano. I paused, realizing I had subconsciously ordered my friend Stephanie's favorite drink. The tattooed barista started to make the drink, wasting no time. I hated americanos, so I did what any mature adult would do and pretended everything was fine by making my way to the seats just outside of view. There was no way I was going to be rude and ask for a different drink.

Cutting my losses I took in the small shop around me. It was practically empty, save for a few people huddled over laptops in the corner.

Feeling the absence of my phone and set on avoiding awkward eye contact—I focused on the decor. The distressed wood walls were covered in old posters and an artist's psychedelic work. Each painting was spread throughout with a price below each piece.

I was inspecting the painting titled *We are the Aliens,* featuring a kaleidoscope of colors intricately mixed throughout each other, when I heard the barista shout my order. I grabbed my coffee and returned to my seat. I didn't touch the bitter all-coffee-no-sugar drink.

I had to go to work early tomorrow, but I couldn't go home. I had embarrassed myself in front of Stephanie, my friend and roommate, with no idea how to face her. I sat there fiddling with my drink internally freaking out until I noticed the barista wiping down a table. Her smile had disappeared completely as she was now shooting me annoyed looks with each wipe of the table. I leaned over peering at the shop hours posted on the door: *6am-10:30pm.* The previous people in the corner were gone, and the clock now read ten-thirty-four. Flustered, I mumbled an apology and hurried out of the shop.

Coffee in hand, I walked slowly down the dimly lit street. I considered my options with Steph, maybe I would just pretend nothing happened, and we would never talk about it again. *Or maybe I could change my name and leave the country.* While contemplating the realities of moving and how difficult it would be to obtain a visa, I heard footsteps behind me. I turned my head discreetly to see who was trailing me. My attention flew to the extra pair of arms the thick figure behind me possessed. Just as I attempted to get a better view, I felt hands grip my wrists.

Coffee splattered across the ground as I thrashed against their tight hold. My hands were pulled behind me, leaving me at a disadvantage. I racked my brain trying to remember what I had learned in the self defense class Steph always dragged me to. She insisted I go after I started online dating, saying it would help her "stress less." A vague memory of a lesson came to mind as I kicked backward. Another hand caught my ankle, forcing me to a full stop. The self defense teacher did not incorporate people with four arms into his teachings. *If I make it out alive, I'm definitely going to ask for my money back.* A kick against the back of my leg sent me to my knees as a second person stepped into view. I looked up into the other captor's face.

Purple skin and four black eyes greeted me. *Not a person, it must be a demon or an alien.* My useless brain decided it was more important to figure out what this creature was instead of the fact I was in deep shit. As I tried to decide whether it was better to get kidnapped by aliens or demons, I felt a pinch against my neck. My muscles gave out and my head flopped forward, limiting my view to the concrete beneath me.

"Now remember Val, if moved to a second location the chance of survival drops dramatically." The words from my self-defense instructor echoed in my head as I hung helplessly. My captors carried me effortlessly up a metal ramp.

Definitely aliens, I decided as I prepared myself for the worst. *Sorry Steph, looks like I won't be able to fix this between us after all.*

She was worried about a bad date taking me, when the real danger was apparently being abducted by fucking aliens. Still unable to move, I was quickly shuttled through a tight hallway. It was lined with a small trail of lights on the floor that cast barely enough light to see. I felt the ground lurch beneath me. My limp limbs swung from the shift, throwing my captors off balance. I begged my muscles to move, to do something while I had the opportunity, but they refused. The aliens steadied themselves and continued to our destination.

We approached the end of the hallway, facing a metal door. As it slid open, the grip on my arm loosened just as I regained control over my body. Before I could even think to run, strong hands pushed me into a dim room.

I fell face first. My body collided with the cool metal floor, knocking the air out of me. The taste of blood filled my mouth as I laid there stunned for a few breaths before I could pull myself up. Pushing to my knees I took in my surroundings. The metal lined room was empty save for a couple of small pads spread throughout. It was lit only by a small blue light fixed to the ceiling, and in the corner three women and one man sat huddled. Their wary eyes all focused on me.

"Another one huh?" A woman with short curly hair spoke. As she made her way over to me, the dim light made the grime on her pink pajamas visible. She hadn't gone down without a fight either. "Welcome to the party," she said, her voice oddly cheery.

"Any idea where we are?" I grasped her hand, letting her pull me up from the floor as she led me over to the group. A couple of sniffles from a petite blonde curled into a ball filled the silence. The short curly-haired woman took a minute to compose her thoughts.

"So far all we've got is that most of us were minding our own business, sleeping, walking to a car, taking the trash out—you know, regular stuff —and next minute, bam! Blacking-out before waking up to being thrown in here by four-armed aliens."

Like the other women, I hadn't even noticed being followed. Of course, I definitely wasn't expecting to get abducted either, let alone by aliens. Letting out a sigh, I looked back up at the group. "Same here. Any idea on where they are taking us?"

Two of the women shook their heads and the petite one let out a sob.

The man's expression was empty. His tank top hung loosely around his impressive muscles as he sat staring at the wall, completely unaware of the conversation going on around him.

"Your guess is as good as ours," a girl with bruises across her brown skin and with long dark bangs chimed in.

"Well let's not think about depressing things like that. I'm Lynn by the way," the woman with the short brown hair said with a smile. "This is Marie," she placed her hand on the petite blond's shoulder. "This is Sara." Sara looked up through her dark bangs at the mention of her name then promptly returned to staring at the floor. "And this is…" Her gaze lingered on the man for a moment, waiting for a response. When she received none, she shrugged and looked back at me.

"I'm Valerie, Val for short," I replied, pulling my legs in tightly.

We all sat in silence for several minutes as if it would help us make sense of our situation. Marie let out a couple more muffled sobs while Lynn rubbed her back cooing, "It's okay. You're not alone," several times.

Noticing Sara's strong gaze, I locked eyes with her. "We've got to get out of here."

"How'd you plan on doing that exactly?"

Taking a minute to think I let my eyes wander. Sara's gaze dropped to her beat-up checkered Vans. She wore black ripped skinny jeans with a band t-shirt and a studded belt around her waist. "What if we use your belt?"

Her brows pinched together as she looked at me. She let out a soft sigh and unbuckled her belt, waiting for an explanation. The two others joined her and the man continued staring at the wall. I swallowed, my nerves acting up now that I was the center of attention. "Okay so, what if we take a hostage?"

"With a belt?" Sara shot me a skeptical glare, making it feel like I just told her that pigs could fly, or that aliens existed. Oh wait, they apparently do.

"Right," I continued, "If we can distract one of those four-arm guys and get him in the room, one of us can get behind him and use the belt to put him in a choke hold. Then we'll negotiate for our freedom in exchange for his safety."

"Girl, you watch too many movies." Lynn snorted and held Marie closer as she continued to let out more sobs.

"Well, does anyone else have a better suggestion?" I threw up my hands challenging everyone till they all averted their gazes.

"I don't want to die," the nameless man mumbled under his breath.

Everyone gave a solemn nod in agreement.

My jaw clenched and I felt the metal studs of the belt dig into my hands. "Well we clearly don't know what these guys want with us. Worst case scenario, they think of humans as some delicacy. Best case, they want a new pet. Whatever it is: We. Are. Fucked." Emphasizing each word I looked back at the group. They all stared back at me, the fear apparent in their eyes.

"You think we don't know that?!" Sara snapped.

"I'm not going down without a fight." I paced the room, the sound of my shoes clanking against the metal filling the silence. The situation finally hit me as I circled the room for the third time. I felt my legs weaken beneath me. I knew I barely had a chance of taking one of these guys down. I'd already attempted and failed.

But I can't give up yet.

"They were supposed to be hot aliens!" Marie let out a wail, throwing her head into her hands.

Jaws dropping and eyebrows raised we all turned towards Marie. With expert precision, Lynn traded her surprise for concern and continued to comfort Marie. "Maybe the next aliens we meet will be hot."

Marie gave Lynn a small nod and a few more sniffles in response. The doors slid open and one of the four-armed aliens shouted something at us in a language we couldn't understand. Startled, we all bunched together hoping for safety in numbers. Unhappy that we couldn't understand, the alien said something that sounded close to a curse and left the room, the sound of the doors locking behind him. We stayed silent for the next several hours.

I had talked a big game but the truth was, I was just as scared as the others.

The next several days followed a pattern. First, breakfast, which consisted of flavorless bars with the texture of compacted sand. The aliens would unceremoniously shove them through a small opening near the door—with only a smack to the metal to notify us of their arrival. Lunch and dinner were the same tasteless meals with no variations.

Luckily our captors decided to provide us with a working toilet and sink located in a separate room giving us some semblance of privacy. Most importantly, the bathroom housed the only window, giving us a glimpse of the inky black emptiness of space around us.

The majority of the group's conversations stayed light, avoiding the heavy topic of our abduction. We eventually found out the man's name was Logan. He had been taken while on his way home from the gym. That was all we learned because Logan was usually silent, never adding much to the discussion. Lynn believed he needed more time, but I think he needed more than that.

I never realized how noisy day to day life had been until now. Only speaking in hushed voices and whispers had made me nostalgic for the background noises of the city. When someone spoke, cried or even snored a couple decibels above whispering, we were hushed in the form of a loud bang from our alien jailers. Luckily they left it at that, not laying a finger on us since the first day.

You'd think with the technology that allowed them to travel to Earth and back, they would have figured out how to block out the noise from a couple humans. But who was I to understand their strange ways when I couldn't even figure out why they'd taken me in the first place.

In between our other conversations, the group quietly theorized how we might escape. Lynn's idea was to talk our way out. That plan didn't work out as well as she hoped, because every time she tried to talk through the door, the aliens would silence her with a smack against the metal.

We had considered plenty of ideas on how to escape the room, but we always came up short of solutions on how to get back to Earth.

After five days in space, tensions were high among the group.

"Alright everyone, we need to do something now." I set down my half eaten sand bar, not having the stomach to choke down the rest.

"Yeah, we need to do something about this awful food," Marie quipped.

Sara rolled her eyes. "We can't just sit around waiting for something to happen, Val and I are ready to act, we just need to know that you two will be with us on this."

"We don't even know how to get back to Earth," Lynn said.

"We'll just have to figure it out, and that's if we even make it that far." I met Lynn's gaze. Dark circles sagged underneath her eyes, and I was sure I looked the same. Sleep was a luxury. Some of us had nightmares and some would just lay awake unable to stifle fears of the unknown. For me, it was the latter.

"Let's think about it a little longer, I don't want to do anything unless we are certain we have a way back." Lynn kept her voice low.

Marie nodded along.

Sara sighed. "We don't have much time, each day we get farther and farther from home."

"I know, but if we act rashly we could make things worse." Lynn turned her head towards the door, making sure we weren't disturbing the sensitive-hearing aliens.

"But if we wait too long it'll be too late," I said, not bothering to hide the anguish in my voice.

The group sat in silence for a moment. The small light cast a sickly blue hue only emphasizing how haggard everyone looked. While I wasn't alone in my worries, it felt like Sara and I were the only ones who felt the urgency of our situation. At the rate we were taking to agree on a plan, we were inching closer and closer to the alien's destination and our potential doom. That was the worst case scenario in my mind.

After the shared silence, Lynn spoke. "Fine, let's go with Val's plan." The optimism had dissipated from Lynn's demeanor days ago. She was finally ready to act.

"Are you with us, Logan?" Sara asked.

He had been the only one not to say anything. He glanced at Sara, giving a noncommittal shrug. That was enough for her and we started to go over the plan again.

The next day I had a difficult time keeping myself from fidgeting. My plan was the one we had decided on, but I was quickly losing confidence. The entire morning consisted of whispers between the group. After the plan was set, an unsettled feeling fell across us. Preparing ourselves for the task ahead of us, we ate breakfast in contemplative silence.

After we finished, we all got into position. Lynn, Marie and Logan stood far from the door, preparing to cause a racket. Even with his height and size being an advantage, Logan had refused to take a position by the door, leaving it to five-foot-two Sarah and me to work as the key figures in the plan. I knew that everyone here was near—or in a state of a mental breakdown, but I couldn't help but feel disappointed in Logan for refusing to help.

Sara and I took our places on either side of the door. Although Sara was smaller than me, she stood confidently with a smile on her face. "I can't wait to see the look on their stupid alien faces when we take them down."

I tried to muster as much bravery as her. Ready with a belt and Sara with shoelaces, we signaled towards Lynn and Marie to begin. They began to scream at the top of their lungs and Logan pounded on the wall. A loud *thunk* hit the doors making them shudder slightly. When the women continued their screaming, another blow to the door landed. Logan quit entirely and the other two lowered their voices, but Sara and I motioned for them to continue. I steadied my breathing in suspense. Not my parents, my ex, nor aliens could trap me.

I will always choose to go down fighting.

The doors slid open with a low hiss, followed by two of the four-armed aliens pacing carefully into the room. They carried what looked eerily similar to guns held close to their bodies. Sara's eyes widened as she took note of the weapons. Taking a breath, I strengthened my resolve and leapt at the alien closest to me. Not much taller, I easily whipped the belt over my head and around the alien's neck. His two free arms flew up to snatch the belt off, but I pulled my arms tighter, gripping the belt as snuggly as possible. Silently applauding myself for succeeding, I looked over the alien's shoulder to see Sara with her hands up as the other alien pointed his gun straight at her heart.

Not ready to give up, I struggled against the alien trying to free himself from my grasp. The two aliens spoke in a language that mostly consisted of S's and clicks, but I could tell the one in my grip was speaking more frantically. The other alien kept his eyes and gun firmly planted on Sara, completely ignoring the struggling alien beneath me. He motioned for her to join the rest of the group in the back and Sara complied.

The trapped alien decided to give up on freeing himself from the belt and instead turned, ramming his back—and me—into the wall. I let out a gasp as my back collided with the barrier, forcing my hands to remain strong against the belt. The alien smashed me into the wall again. My grip began to slip.

"Help!" I cried.

After the third hit, I lost hold of the belt entirely. Falling to the ground, my back throbbed as I struggled to return to my feet. The freed alien turned towards me. I crawled backwards. My legs scrambled as I tried to get as far away as possible. His feet thudded against the metal as he approached. With my back pressed against the wall, there was nowhere left to run. I looked around frantically, locking eyes with each member of the group on the other side of the room.

"Please, we have to fight," I begged.

The alien stood over me, anger flashing in his face. The group turned away when his gun handle smashed against my head.

TWO

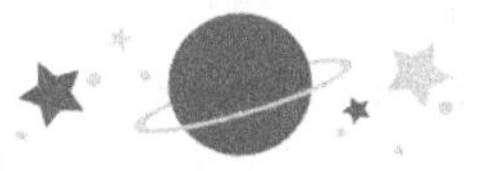

Star System 86

TE'RYN

"Are you sure you have to go?" The human woman with large brown eyes looked up at me as I stood up from the sofa.

"I wish I could stay, but I'm a busy man."

"Well, I hope you'll visit again soon." She stood up, wrapping a golden robe around her to protect from the cool breeze blowing through the open arches that lined the room. The shimmering fabric draped against her body, accentuating each of her curves.

"I could be convinced," I said, leaning a hand against the sofa. I took a moment to take in the beautiful scene. If I were an artist I would paint this moment to capture it in its entirety. The view through the open arches of the room gave us an unfiltered view of the two suns setting across the multi-colored fields of Grihan. The sunlight danced on the female's pink skin, making it look as if she glowed. I was almost inclined to believe the high cost of visiting the human was fair.

Almost.

Humans were quickly becoming a favorite among Alderian males, and I was no exception. Their colorful eyes, the various shades of their skin and their perfect small features left nothing to be desired.

"Was I not convincing enough?" she asked, turning. The light from the sunset caught her eyes, shifting the brown to amber.

"Convincing as silversalt." I poured myself another drink, not removing my gaze.

"Isn't that a drug?"

"Mhmm, a very addicting one too."

She giggled and poured herself another drink.

"Could I ask you for one more favor before I go?" Setting my cup down I considered running my fingers through her silky black hair. *Would it feel similar to mine?* This past hour had cost more credits than I would need to eat for a year, I didn't want to add another unnecessary charge on top of it.

"And what would that be? One more round?" She smirked. Another human term, but I could guess the meaning.

"Yes, if you could so kindly grab another bottle of Korop I would love to share one last drink with you." I finished the last of the drink in my hand and shook the empty bottle for emphasis.

"You weren't difficult to convince at all." Her smile finally reached her eyes. I knew humans weren't here by choice, but they were quite good at pretending to be interested in all the males that came here to spend time in their company.

I leaned in, meeting her gaze. "Just one more round then I'll have to get back to work."

"*Eye contact: twenty credits.*" The small screen on the table chimed, adding to my growing tab.

Vaat.

"Doctor work?" Her eyebrow raised slightly.

"Yes, exactly. It's a tough profession, but seeing my patients heal is its own reward."

"Alright, that will be two-hundred more credits."

"Of course," I gave her another smile as I set up a transfer through my palmpad. "For the afternoon with me, and for the extra drink." I held out my hand waiting for her to initiate the transfer. She looked at my hand, recognition flashing across her face.

"Pay here." She slid the small screen across the table. I touched my palm to the screen until it chimed, indicating the transfer had gone through. I felt a part of my soul leave along with the large amount of credits.

"I'll be right back with that drink." With one last smile she turned and exited the room.

I waited till the sound of her footsteps disappeared down the hallway. Once I was sure she was gone, I made my way to the door, checking my palmpad before I left.

"*Vaat.*" I let out another curse as I assessed my credits.

With how much that pretty human's time had cost I would break about even on this mission. Humans were rare. It was illegal to travel to their star system as the Federation had put a ban on the developing species' planet. That didn't stop the greedy traders though. If a crew could retrieve and sell a human, they would be set for life. The only difficult part was the journey. Getting to their star systems was a long and expensive trek that many couldn't make. But once there, it was easy to capture one; the tiny humans were defenseless against the strength and technology of the many races throughout the galaxies, making them easy targets.

The want for humans had only grown after their discovery. No Alderian male could resist the allure of large eyes, intoxicating scent and curvy bodies. Bolxi, the owner of the Grihan pleasure house, took advantage of that. She created a monopoly on the trade of humans, making it so they could only be found here, causing demand as well as her credits to grow.

Stepping out into the hall, I tapped the thin silver hologram ring around my neck. I waited a moment for it to work to completely obscure my features. Once I was assured it was working properly, I gently pushed open the heavy wooden door of the next room over. The target, Vish'groth Al Dyn, a senator of the Alderian empire, stood in the bathroom. He was occupied at the sink splashing water on his face. It took a moment for him to register my presence. Catching my face in the reflection of the mirror, he spoke, "Good, you're here D'itri. I told you you'd enjoy your time here."

I kept quiet. While I made sure to wear the same long silver robes as D'itri, and now had his face projected on mine, I didn't think to prepare the necessary tool to change my voice.

I wasn't planning on chatting anyways.

D'itri must've not been much of a talker, because Vish'groth returned to washing his face not waiting for an answer. I slowly made my way over to him. With one last splash of water across his face he reached over, tapping the counter till he found a towel, bringing it up to his face.

Pulling a black dagger from my hip, in a familiar motion I plunged it through his back straight into his heart. Vish'groth fell to his knees, only a gurgle escaping his lips. I twisted the knife for good measure. Pulling it free, I wiped the dark blood off onto his Amaxian silk blouse. Over twenty-thousand credits spent on that silk, only to end up covered by his own blood. I considered the possibility of taking the remaining unsoiled silk but decided against it. *Best not to have anything tying me to the scene.* Sliding my dagger back into its sheath with a *click*, I stepped out of the room checking if the hall was empty.

"Heading out already?" The human's voice echoed down the hallway.

I stopped. My fingers twitched at my side as I considered what I might have to do. I tapped the ring around my neck quickly shifting the hologram back to Dr. Fet'lan's face.

"Unfortunately I have to get back to work. Enjoy that drink on my behalf." I adjusted my robe, trying to seem casual.

"Good luck with your work. Make sure to stop by again, Dr. Fet'lan."

I gave the human a small nod before setting off towards my ship and my next target.

THREE

Star System 2047

VAL

Head pounding, I pulled myself off the cool metal floor. "Me and this floor are getting to know each other a little too well." I groaned as I forced my sore muscles to move.

A low chuckle sounded from across the dark room. I froze. My eyes snapped up as I took in my surroundings, trying to find the source of the sound.

I had been moved to another room entirely.

It contained a small blue light similar to the other room, though this light was dimmer, leaving most of the room covered in darkness. Stacked metal crates lined the walls. Next to a stack sat a large form obscured by the shadows. I felt my breath catch as I took in the figure before me as he stepped into the light. Rising to his full height, he stood a good two feet above me. A large scar stretched across his left cheek up to his eye. My heart skipped a beat as I took in his dark gray skin and silver eyes. If I were color blind I could have thought of him as a large human, but he was very much an alien.

"*Diti an' varrsht*," he said, stepping towards me.

I took a step back. "Sorry, I don't understand."

"*Vaat.*" His deep voice rumbled as he took another step forward.

I took another step backwards. My back met the wall, leaving me cornered. He took a moment to assess me, then held his hands up in a placating gesture. Bending down he grabbed a tray of thc sand bars off thc floor, holding it out to me like some sort of peace offering.

"Ue'li." He held the tray out farther. His eyes flicked between me and the food. Minutes passed in the stand down between us. Not wanting to make the huge gray alien upset, I gingerly reached for a bar.

"Mmm, love this stuff," I said, flashing him a cheesy grin.

He let out a snort and set the tray back down.

"Wait, do you understand me?" I asked, setting down the unfinished bar. Even the possibility of an angry alien couldn't make me eat anymore of the stuff.

He nodded and tapped his right ear twice.

Straining to see in the dim light, I leaned slightly forward. Noticing my attention, he turned, giving a view of a small silver cylinder wedged into his ear canal.

"Is that a translator?" I leaned in further trying to get a better view.

He nodded again.

"Are you a captive too?"

"*Dal*." he said with a nod.

"Do you know where we are?"

He took a second to think then shook his head. "*Vir*."

That must mean no. Okay so far so good, I thought. We got the basics down, and he seemed friendly. Hopefully he would be able to enlighten me about the current situation.

"Do you know the four-arm guys? Where they're taking us? What they want with us?" I spoke a mile a minute, the questions plaguing me tumbling out.

He held up a hand to stop me, then pointed to himself. "J'tan." He pointed to me and raised his eyebrows.

"Oh sorry, I should have introduced myself first before asking a million questions. I'm Val." I held out my hand. He looked a bit puzzled, still keeping his distance.

Waiting.

I quickly returned my hand to my side,

cheeks flushing with embarrassment. *Of course an alien wouldn't know what a handshake is.*

"Val," he said, chuckling as he repeated my name.

"Oh god, hopefully it doesn't mean something stupid in your language."

He let out a bellowing laugh, his chest heaving as he tried to contain it.

"I'll take that as a yes," I muttered, my cheeks fully red.

DAYS TURNED into weeks and weeks into months as the monotony blurred everything together. I wondered if Steph would report my absence. Not that it would do any good, but still I wondered how long it would take for the police and Steph to give up looking for me. It still hurt to think about her. She was the one who took me in after my break up with Robert. I had lived with him since I was eighteen and everything we had was under his name, leaving me with nothing but the clothes on my back when we split four years ago.

Without any help from my family, Steph let me move in, set me up with a coding program and I was able to get my first job. Thanks to her, I had finally gotten my life together. I was finally happy. Then I had to go and ruin it all with my late night trip to the coffee shop just to avoid an awkward conversation. I had to get back home, even if it was only to clear things up with Steph.

Each day followed the same routine. Sand bars for every meal and language lessons from J'tan. The lessons mostly consisted of me asking in English and when that didn't translate, I would draw poor imitations of objects in the scattered sand from my many uneaten bars. The several weeks with nothing else to do gave me the time and motivation I needed to pick up the new language.

From what I could understand, J'tan came from a planet called Aldar. He worked as a bounty hunter and was on a mission to stop the four-armed aliens—Azzeks. Visiting my star system—the human star system—was apparently illegal and J'tan could have gotten a large sum of money for turning the Azzeks in. But his plan failed as he ended up as their captive instead. His use of many curse words made his anger apparent every time the topic came up. I asked him many questions about his world and the other nearby worlds that contained all kinds of different alien species. However, every time I brought up the topic of mine and the other human's fates he would quickly change the subject.

After receiving dinner, I crushed up a bar on

the tray, thinking of what I could draw to learn the words of next. I set it in the usual spot waiting for J'tan. Yesterday he had tried, and failed, to explain the many foods they ate on his planet. He got frustrated quickly and just left it at how I would have to see for myself to understand. Patience wasn't the large aliens' strong suit, but he was starting to grow on me. Grumpiness and all.

CLANKS AND CURSES sounded from the restroom. "Everything okay in there?" I stood by the bathroom door, not sure what to do if J'tan wasn't okay. *Does CPR even work on aliens?*

"Yeah, I'm just fixing the sink, it's not working great."

I opened the door, and J'tan was on his back underneath the small metal sink welded to the wall. He was fiddling with the pipes underneath.

"Why are you even bothering to fix it? If anything we should be trashing all the Azzek's stuff."

"Fixing stuff just helps me clear my mind, and we still need to use it after all."

After a couple more clunks J'tan stood and checked the result of his work. The water ran smoothly instead of the slow trickles I had become accustomed to. Satisfied with the result, J'tan wiped his hands on his black pants and exited the bathroom, noting the tray on the ground. "Eat—you'll need the energy. We'll be arriving soon."

My head whipped around. "To where they'll be dropping us off?" I asked, failing to keep calm and botching several Alderian words in the process.

"Yes, and we will part ways," he said, pushing the tray towards me.

"What do you mean?"

"Don't worry little one, you'll be taken care of."

I noted his use of the phrase *take care of*, often used alongside words like *baby*, or *animal*. Anger bubbling inside me, I turned towards him. "Don't you have a plan to escape or something? Let me help!"

He put a hand on my shoulder and met my eyes. "You'll have food and shelter, a tiny human like you will be safe there."

"And where is there?" I forced out the words as calmly as I could muster.

"Grihan," he replied, leaving it at that. He laid down resting his arms behind his head. His silent way of saying, *conversation over.*

"J'tan please," I begged.

"Sorry little one," he replied, turning his back to me.

I stomped towards him. "And what is on Grihan?"

Silence.

"What is on Grihan?" I repeated through gritted teeth.

J'tan let out a breath. "A pleasure house."

My stomach dropped. "You're just going to let them take us there?"

"The planet is beautiful and they take care of humans there. You'll want for nothing."

"Nothing but my freedom."

J'tan ignored my comment, closing his eyes.

I tossed and turned for hours that night. Giving up on attempting to sleep I stared at the metal ceiling above me. My chance of escaping had become even more of an impossible task. Even with the support of the other women, we still failed to do something other than mildly inconvenience the Azzeks. J'tan seemed entirely unbothered by his situation. He obviously had something in mind, I just had to figure out what it was.

I considered my options with our impending arrival. I could keep trying to convince J'tan to fill me in on what he planned to do when we landed. That possibility seemed unlikely with his stoic behavior, but·maybe if I persisted long enough I might succeed in swaying him. Alternatively, I could just play along nicely, lulling the Azzeks into a false sense of security.

Then I could make a break for it while they tried to transfer me. Then of course, there was the added problem of getting the other women out. Overwhelmed with the unknown, I laid awake thinking through every scenario.

J'tan's whisper broke the silence. I listened closely, eavesdropping on his conversation.

"We'll arrive in four rotations," he paused. "They've got a bunch of humans on here."

My heart pounded against my chest. I focused on keeping my breathing steady to avoid drawing J'tan's attention.

"Yeah I know, it's not worth it. I'll let you know when we land, so you can get me out of here." A small beep sounded and he let out a sigh. He made his way back to his sleep area, keeping his footsteps light to avoid waking me.

After hearing his soft snores, I returned to my normal breathing. J'tan was planning on escaping and I was going with him, whether he liked it or not.

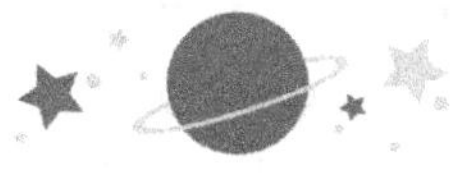

FOUR

Star System 73

VAL

The next couple days were filled with one word conversations and awkward silences. J'tan would attempt to say something, but I always cut him short. Still feeling the sting from the betrayal, I couldn't muster the energy to fake any interest in what he had to say. I knew J'tan owed me nothing, but I had at least thought I'd formed something of a friendship with the grumpy alien.

On the fourth day of my imposed silent treatment, I felt the ship come to a stop. Catching my balance, I waited with bated breath watching the door for the Azzeks. A couple of hours passed with no sign of anyone coming to collect us. I turned to J'tan, breaking my silence. "Where are they? Didn't we land?"

"They're probably unloading the more

compliant passengers first," he said with a slight smirk.

After learning more of his language, one of his first questions was why had I been moved into a room with him. He didn't understand why the Azzeks would risk their 'expensive cargo' like that. Leaving me with someone who had fought them and could be considered dangerous—was a risky move in his mind. I filled him in about our attempted escape and my failure at taking one of the Azzeks down. Upon hearing my story, J'tan spat out all of his food in a fit of laughter. Shortly after, he promptly gave me several rough pats, congratulating me for getting the drop on the Azzeks and cracking my back in return.

The sound of several footsteps filled the halfway. I waited for the sound of the doors opening. What I heard instead was a loud *thud*, followed by several curses. After a couple more thuds, the door slid open. The door hung off kilter and shuddered as it came to a stop.

On the other side stood two tall thin aliens with blue skin and yellow eyes. One, most likely a male with his sharper features, kept his forest green hair cropped short with the sides shaved. The other had softer features, leading me to believe she was a female. She sported a long braided ponytail as well as a massive gun that she carried with both hands. *These are the hot aliens Marie wanted.*

"You really thought you could take on a whole ship of Azzeks huh? Is this what Aerix would have wanted?" The one with cropped-hair said, a hint of anger tinging his voice.

I could have sworn I saw J'tan's eyes mist up. His hand covered the small pendant he wore around his neck, a motion I'd grown familiar with in the time we spent together. He had said nothing about the pendant when I asked, adding more to the growing list of things I didn't know about him. He blinked, removing any evidence as quickly as it appeared.

"No." he replied.

The ponytail alien's gaze met mine then turned to J'tan, changing the topic. "Is this the human you were talking about?"

"Yeah, took the poor thing straight from her planet." A look of sympathy crossed his face.

My lungs filled with air in preparation of all the pent up anger I had to share.

"Let's go before more of the Azzek bastards show up," the cropped-hair alien said, his eyes scanning the hallway.

I opened my mouth to speak and before I could say anything, J'tan interjected. "Sorry little one, in this universe you gotta look out for yourself."

My lungs deflated in defeat. *Looks like I'm going with plan C.* I made a split-second decision and spun towards the open door and ran.

As I made my way towards the hall, the cropped-hair alien moved in front of me, blocking my way. I slid straight into him, unable to change directions in such a short amount of time.

"Nuh-uh, little human, you're staying here. No way we can afford the repercussions of being seen with you."

Ignoring him, I feinted left then stepped towards the right. I made it two steps around him before he grabbed me with strong hands.

"Look, you don't need to be seen with me, just let me go!" I struggled against his grip. *Why are aliens so strong?*

"You wouldn't last a rotation out there Val. Just stay here." J'tan gave my shoulder a light pat in an attempt to soothe me. My eyes met his, my anger rising. I shook his hand off my shoulder. Not helping me was one thing but keeping me here was something I couldn't forgive.

He pulled me backwards with a swift jerk. As my butt hit the ground, I watched as he and the other aliens left. The door, and my chance of escape closed behind them.

I slid down to the ground laying on my back. "At least you're reliable," I said, patting the floor.

The tears I held back for so long finally broke free. I didn't know if minutes or hours had passed, and at this point I couldn't bring myself to care. No matter how much I tried to power through the fear and uncertainty, only focusing on the goal—nothing had worked in the end. Even the years of self-defense training had all been for nothing. The only thing I had received from those classes was a false sense of comfort. *Maybe it's time to throw in the towel.*

I heard the doors open and footsteps approach, but I didn't move. Even when I felt the grip of hands pulling me off the floor, I didn't struggle. Pulled to my feet, I saw the familiar silhouette of a four-armed alien. A black visor now obscured his face. With a tug on my arm I followed compliantly, shifting my gaze back down to the floor in defeat. A swinging gun holstered to the Azzek's waist caught my attention. Mustering my last bit of courage, I grabbed it with my free hand. By the time the alien noticed, it was too late. Pulling the trigger, I swung the gun upwards. The alien caught the gun by the barrel, as a blast flew past him bashing a crate behind us.

Bang!

The room shook and the Azzek and I were thrown back from the explosion. I let out a cry as my shoulder smashed against the wall. Alarms blared, and smoke filled the room. Coughing, I pushed myself up with my good arm taking in the destruction around me. The room was in shambles. Crates were blasted apart and a large hole remained where a wall once had been. *This is my chance.* I stood, scanning the room. The Azzek laid face down, unmoving. I stepped cautiously over the debris taking in the sight through the gaping hole.

Hundreds of spaceships of various sizes sat still as if held by invisible strings. Ramps stretched out to each ship from doors speckled across a massive wall of orange tinted glass. The entirety of the area was surrounded by a translucent half-cylinder that kept the black of space at bay.

Shouts filled the outside of the ship and various aliens of all shapes sizes, arm count and colors stared at the source of the explosion. Some of the onlookers shouted in languages I couldn't understand, but most looked on in curious silence. Before the bug-eyes of an alien could meet mine, I ducked down.

J'tan and his friends clearly wanted to avoid being seen with a human. I'd have to play this smart if I didn't want to go from one captor to another. Crawling back over to the Azzek, I gave him a gentle nudge. He was out cold.

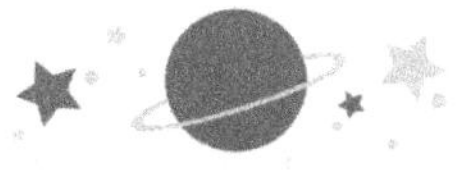

FIVE

Star System 73

TE'RYN

"Vaat, I hate this shit-hole of a station," I muttered under my breath as I stepped in *another* puddle of mysterious liquid.

The contact I was on my way to see had asked to meet here. The old space station in Star System Seventy-Three was one of the more seedy locations in the galaxies. The station sat on an asteroid, falling on the outskirts of the Federation and the Renari Empire, leaving it out of the jurisdiction of both powers. It was the perfect location for all the dealings of the underworld, as neither governing forces had the power to enforce their laws here.

This client was rumored to be a snob—so I splurged on my outfit. Dressing to impress. Unfortunately after this, I would have to discard my new boots. I learned the hard way in the past that nothing could get this disgusting station goo out.

Two hundred credits down the drain. I sighed at the thought.

The smell of silversalt smoke filled the air as I approached the small bar that sat at the back of the station. I stepped around the various races filling the room as I continued on my way to the bartender.

"One glass of Korop." I tapped the counter, transferring my credits. With a grunt, the bartender hit a button causing the glass to ascend from a hole in the counter. I retracted my helmet, downing the drink in one swig. I returned my helmet quickly, not wanting to choke on the smoke and the lack of air. When the mining station in Star System Seventy-Three was abandoned, the equipment to keep the air supply going fell into disrepair, forcing the shadier inhabitants to wear oxygen masks at all times. No one seemed to mind though, it was easier to conceal your identity this way.

I made my way to the booths in the back. Broken lights made the booths appear even more decrepit, something I didn't think was possible in this place. Sure, the ambience of the worn furniture and the smoke of several drugs —banned in every other planet across the galaxy—made it perfect for shady deals with various skilled characters of the underworld.

But there were much classier places to make a deal.

I slid into the booth facing my new client. He had spared no expense on his outfit either. Gaudy colors clashed together underneath a long veil that covered his face—an attempt to prevent any chance of recognition.

It was a wasted effort. The veil couldn't hide the signature horns of the Renari race. Notwithstanding, I had already used my intel to find out who I'd be working for. *I don't just work for anyone after all.* He was just another prince vying for the throne. I'd gotten several requests after the death of the Renari monarch, but this one had offered the highest bid.

"Who sings the Dallith song?" He asked.

Ugh, why does everyone have to be so dramatic with their code words? "A friend," I replied, adding a smile for good measure.

"Welcome. I trust you know what I ask?"

"Yeah yeah, all I need is payment." I held out my hand.

He pulled a chip out of his long sleeves and handed it to me. I inspected it, a kureis chip— untrackable, good. I gave him a nod and stood. "I'll notify you when it's done."

I stood from the booth, the old furniture creaking once free of my weight. I gave the prince one last look and left the bar, walking at a brisk pace through the poorly lit halls, not even slowing to avoid puddles. The sooner I got out of this place, the better. Females and males called to me as I pushed on through the larger hallways of the station. The orange lights from their small rooms filled the hallway advertising their professions—enticing me to spend the next hours in ecstasy. But I ignored them, I had a job to do after all.

Before I could step out onto the docks, a loud explosion shook the bay. Following the source of the blast, I spotted the cause. A ship sporting a large hole in its exterior sat smoking in a bay nearby. Several Azzeks yelled, rushing from the doors of another vessel towards the smoldering ship. On the other side of the hole stood another Azzek. Its suit was singed, but it seemed otherwise unharmed from the blast. I watched as it made its way out of the hole. The legs of the suit were too long, fabric catching on the Azzek's feet as it clumsily tried to climb down the outside of the ship.

"I wonder if it's injured," an onlooker commented.

The Azzek took its time climbing down, cautiously testing each step and only using two of its four arms.

"Vaat, Azzeks can't even build ships right," another onlooker spat.

Noticing the group of Azzeks running to the fuming ship, the injured Azzek decided against climbing and lept towards the ramp. I held my breath as I watched the injured Azzek barely bridge the gap, landing with an ungraceful roll. It quickly scrambled to its feet, watching the racket of Azzeks running towards it. Turning away from its crewmates, the Azzek took off down the ramp, stopping only to catch its breath a safe distance away.

"Found the source of the explosion," The onlooker laughed.

I couldn't help laughing either. No one would blame the Azzek for running. That Azzek would have to work the rest of its life to make up for that mistake.

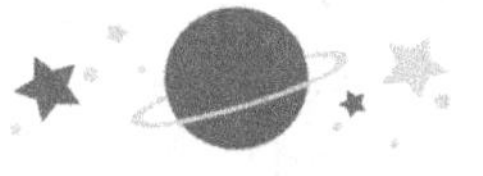

SIX

Star System 73

VAL

I ran till my lungs burned. *In this universe you gotta look out for yourself.* The words from J'tan replayed in my head. I sent a silent apology to the other women. There was nothing I could do. Finally, I stopped, checking behind me for any pursuers. Not seeing any Azzeks following me, I paused to catch my breath. *Maybe I didn't think this through.* I started to panic, gasping for breaths. My lungs struggled to fill. I pulled off the visor panting for more air, but my lungs contracted as I took in a breath. Really panicking now, I returned the visor and forced myself to slow my breathing. *Azzeks must need less oxygen.* I was beginning to believe humans were not made for this side of the galaxy, but I just had to stay calm. Just had to keep going. I pushed forward, taking slow, deep breaths. *You've got this, Val.* With all odds against me, I somehow managed to make it off the ship.

"Hell yeah!" I gave myself a high-five—not caring how cheesy it was. I just made the escape of a lifetime. Maybe that would teach those assholes not to mess with humans again. Without the threat of being captured, I took the time to fully take in my surroundings.

It was like being in a sci-fi movie. Ships left and entered the bay at a consistent rate. Each dock was bustling with aliens filtering to and from vessels of various sizes. Leaning on the railing, I looked to the lower decks.

Below me, two slender aliens with blue skin and dark green hair moved metal crates into an older looking ship—conversing rapidly in a language I couldn't understand. The other ships around them sat empty, the majority of the action reserved for the upper docks. So far my only plan had been to escape. Now that I'd achieved that, I had absolutely no idea where to go from here.

I kept my eyes on the blue aliens as I considered my next steps. One dropped a crate, drawing my full attention. The other alien shouted, finishing with a swift kick to the clumsy alien's knee—dropping him to the floor. A large, dark-gray Alderian marched over to the two arguing aliens. Grabbing them both by the scruff, he knocked their heads together.

I let out a laugh. *Guess aliens aren't too different from humans after all.* Once the fight was settled, the Alderian returned to his conversation. He conversed with a squat alien whose too-large-eyes and ears dwarfed its tiny head. From this angle I could see a large scar stretching across the Alderian's cheek underneath his visor. I inspected the blue aliens further. One had cropped hair and the other a long braided ponytail.

J'tan.

I felt a smile stretch across my face. *Time to improvise.*

I made my way down to the lower docks, making sure to keep a safe enough distance away from J'tans crew. Once below their ship I followed the zig-zag pattern of the docks, and after ascending several stairs I sat just out of eyesight. I watched from below as the blue aliens carried more cargo into the ship, this time without any fighting. J'tan stood with his back facing the ship, still engrossed in conversation with the large-eyed alien.

Counting the time it took them to get in and out of the ship, I estimated I had about a four-minute window. I eyed a large crate and dashed up the stairs once I saw the blue aliens enter the ship. Grabbing the lid, I heaved it open, thanking the universe it wasn't sealed.

The inside of the crate was full of various

types of fabrics. More confused about J'tan's profession, I pushed them aside and slid ungracefully into the crate, making sure to close the lid as gently as possible.

J'tan had been kind to me when I was held captive. While I didn't know where he was going, I was certain it would be better than my original intended destination. I shuddered. If I had it my way, I would never set foot on the planet Grihan. I waited with bated breath till I felt the crate move around me. I could hear muffled arguing from the aliens carrying the crate. I just hoped they wouldn't check to see why it was suddenly heavier. After a few minutes, the crate dropped to the floor with a *thud*. I slapped my hand to my mouth, covering the gasp of surprise that nearly escaped. The sound of footsteps and squabbling eventually dissipated. Once gone, I let out a breath and removed the sweltering visor from my face, grateful I could finally breathe normally. *So far so good.*

About an hour later I felt the engines roar to life, sending a rumble through the ground. I massaged my cramped legs. I couldn't hide in here forever, I'd eventually have to make myself known. But just to be safe, I'd wait till we were far away from the Azzeks.

A computer voice spoke in Alderian over an

intercom. "Preparing to jump, please make sure all passengers are secured."

I pushed my legs against the crate bracing myself.

"One passenger remains unsecured. Jump will not commence until everyone is safely secured," the computer repeated.

"*Vaat*!" Footsteps pounded and J'tan shouted, "I know you're in there, you filthy stowaway! Come out now before I blast every one of these crates apart."

Heart pounding, I lifted the lid.

"Hey J'tan," I said softly, putting on my best smile.

J'tan stood on the other side of a cargo bay flanked by the two blue aliens, each holding large guns. J'tan's hand flew to his forehead and back out in my direction. "Val, what are you doing here?"

I took a moment to respond, trying to figure out what to say. "I may have, uh…caused an explosion." I looked down at the stolen outfit I wore.

The alien with cropped hair doubled over laughing. "J'tan this is too good! Can we keep her?"

"She's not a pet, Avi," J'tan grumbled.

I stopped myself from nodding along with J'tan. Avi seemed like my best chance of convincing him. Even the alien with the ponytail had a slight smirk on her face.

Avi gestured to the ponytail alien. "See, even Evi is amused!"

"Anyone who causes an explosion on an Azzek ship is someone I'd share a drink with," Evi replied.

J'tan paced around, his brows furrowed. "Get her out of those Amaxian silks before she ruins them. I promised we would transport them untouched."

Avi approached and held out his hand. I took it and climbed out of the crate.

J'tan stopped abruptly then looked at me. "We don't take freeloaders around here, you'll have to prove yourself."

"I'll make sure you don't regret it!" I said, beaming.

J'tan turned away, stomping out of the room. "I already am."

"Welcome to the team, little human." Avi smiled.

"Thanks, I'm Val by the way." I unzipped the stolen suit, letting the thoroughly destroyed fabric drop to the ground. When it hit the floor, the several orbs I used to fill the two extra sleeves spilled out. Avi and Evi jumped back, their eyes wide.

"Woah, watch out!" Avi inched farther away

from the orbs, looking as if I had unleashed thousands of spiders on him.

I looked around nervously. "Watch out for what?"

"Care to tell us why you have a suit full of bombs?" Evi asked calmly.

My face paled. I had been running around with not just one, but sixteen bombs shoved into the sleeves of my suit. "I was just trying to make the sleeves look more full."

Avi's laugh filled the room, melting away the tension. "I have a feeling our lives just got a lot more interesting."

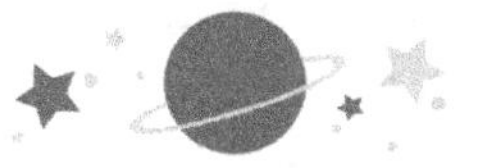

SEVEN

Star System 10

VAL

While the movies made space travel look exciting, they failed to mention how much maintenance went into keeping a spaceship functional. Although not interesting enough to put in any film, it was necessary. Especially with *The Revenge*—the ship J'tan, Avi and Evi lived on. I didn't know much about spaceships, but I could tell from the mismatched patchwork metal and rusted grates, that the ship had seen better days.

J'tan didn't waste any time putting me to work. After a night's rest in a room with an actual bed—the one thing I was the most grateful for—I was given my first task. I was to use my small human stature to squeeze into the air ducts and clean. I'd promised I would make myself useful, so I got straight to work. I spent the next several days trying to scrape off the grime that had accumulated over several years.

The monotony of cleaning brought back the memories of scrubbing toilets at Bible camp. After my parents found my not-so-secret internet search—of whether or not it was okay to like boys *and* girls—they shipped me off to find Jesus in nature. It turned out I just found a troubled teenage boy instead. That's where I met Robert, my ex. I wondered if by now my face was plastered all over the news, and if he'd even taken the time to recognize me. Would my parents feel guilty for not talking to me for ten years? Would they at least pretend to be sad? Most likely they'd blame it on me being led astray and not following the Commandments like they'd wanted. I wondered if there was a space Jesus, maybe I'd find him on the other side of the universe after all.

After my hands felt raw, and my injured shoulder was screaming in agony, I threw my clear, too-large gloves aside, crawling out of the air duct to take a breath of non-dusty air. I gulped down a drink of water. *Almost finished with task one. The next one better be less gross.* There were worse places to be, I understood that. But surely I could do something else. I sat, taking in the state of my clothes. The modified jumpsuit Evi had lent me was now covered in a thick coat of grime, turning the gray to a gross black.

"Done yet?" Avi asked.

I jumped, spilling water across my lap. I hadn't even heard him approach. "Almost." I stood trying to wipe the last of the water off, smearing the grime farther across my pants.

"Good. Next we need you to clean the *Hefsof* chamber." Avi's lips curled up as he watched my reaction carefully.

I didn't know what a *Hefsof* chamber was, and after seeing Avi's mischievous smile, I was sure I never wanted to learn. "Don't you have a cleaning robot or something? I'm sure I'd be more useful doing something else."

I tried to think of skills that might be useful to the crew. I had a certificate in computer science, but the technology here was so vastly different I wouldn't even know where to start. It didn't help that the crew made sure to keep me away from anything more technologically advanced than a bucket and rag. *Maybe I could impress them with my crochet?* I kept myself from smiling at that scenario.

"You said you wanted to pay your way through working on this ship, so that's what we're doing—giving you work. I mean, we could just drop you off at the next planet if that's what you want." Avi emphasized the last sentence.

Of course that was the last thing I wanted and he knew it. I pushed a sarcastic remark to the back of my mind and focused on making friends, not enemies. Last time I'd been a smart-ass at Bible camp, telling the advisor where exactly they could stick their rules, I was put on toilet duty for an entire month. I wasn't about to repeat that mistake.

I kept my voice as sweet as possible. "Once I'm done with the air ducts, can you please show me where the *Hefsof* chamber is?"

"Sure, I'd love to," Avi stopped mid-turn then made eye contact. "Oh, and I forgot to mention, we'll be docking soon and J'tan said you are to remain on the ship—unseen." With that he left as quietly as he came.

Just as Avi had said, I felt the ship come to a stop shortly after finishing my water. Using that as an excuse to end my cleaning for the day, I walked back through the halls, counting the doors till I reached the room the crew had designated as mine. The room was small, only allowing enough space for a small bed and a desk that was welded to the wall. I didn't mind, because this room also came with its own bathroom—including a shower.

Using a sink on the Azzek ship had only done so much for my hygiene. My first night here, I spent at least two hours under the hot water, washing months of filth away. *I'll have to spend longer than that to get the grime of the air ducts off.*

I took my time in the shower. As I lathered

shampoo scented with unfamiliar spices into my hair, suddenly my feet lifted off the ground. I gripped the walls trying to keep myself upright as my body rose towards the ceiling. Legs flailing, I slammed the air dry button. The jets of air only dried half of my body. Shampoo suds floated around my still wet hair. Luckily I had brought clothes into the bathroom. I swam my way through the air managing to grasp a floating clean jumpsuit and pull it on. I pushed against the ceiling till my foot could reach the pad to open the door. "Hello! Your gravity is broken!" I shouted as my back met the ceiling of my bedroom.

I'd always wanted to know what zero gravity felt like, but finding out in the middle of a shower was not how I would have liked my first experience to go.

The smooth wall made it difficult to grab onto anything. It took me a moment to find my space-legs, but after getting used to the sensation, I was able to make it over to a wall. I continued to use the surfaces around me to push my body, attempting to reach the pad to open the door to the hall. On the fourth try, I finally managed to open the door. I angled my feet and rocketed off the wall through the entrance, starting to get the hang of zero gravity. All my dreams of flying as a kid were somehow, in a weird alien way, coming true.

"*Revenge*, gravity on," J'tan's voice echoed from outside.

My body slammed against the floor, knocking the air out of me. My injured shoulder throbbed even more. *Never mind, I definitely do not like zero gravity.*

Evi's laugh echoed throughout the hallway. "You don't even know how to handle zero gravity? Humans are such-"

"Evi, go over the next bounty with Avi," J'tan said, cutting Evi off.

Tears pricking at my eyes, I kept my head on the ground. *It's just from the pain of belly flopping on solid metal, nothing to do with looking dumb.* I lied to myself.

Evi muttered something about J'tan ruining the fun under her breath before she made her way down the hallway. I waited till the last of her footsteps disappeared before I looked up, pushing the soapy wet hair out of my face as J'tan crouched nearby. His gray eyes were full of concern. "Undrians value strength over everything else." He held his hand out.

I stood, ignoring his offered help entirely. "I don't know if you noticed, but humans aren't very strong." I looked away from J'tan feeling ashamed.

"Physically? No. But I know you've got something else in there Val, or else you wouldn't be here. I can see that but you'll have to prove it to the other two before they'll accept you."

"I've been cleaning just as you guys asked. I don't know exactly what else I can do."

J'tan let out a sigh, and rubbed the back of his neck. He didn't seem to know either. "You're a liability, a huge one. If the Federation found out you were here, we would lose our bounty hunter licenses. This job is all Evi and Avi have. Make yourself worth the risk."

I couldn't look J'tan in the eye. I didn't know what I could offer these three. I gave him a solemn nod in reply, and returned to my bedroom.

Later that evening, the sounds of conversation echoed down the hallway reaching my room. Unable to sleep, I tried to make out the muffled words.

No luck.

Curious as to what the other three were talking about, I crept my way out of my bedroom and towards the origin of the voices. I reached the cafeteria and stood outside in the hall peeking my head into the room. Avi, J'tan and Evi all huddled around a hologram of an anthropomorphic cat. Goggles sat on top of the gray patched fur enlarging his yellow slitted eyes, and making the cat-man look even more ridiculous.

"Merrick was last seen on the planet of

Yoru, his bounty is currently sitting at fifteen-thousand credits," J'tan informed the others.

"This is too easy. I already found the shuttle he will be on tomorrow," Evi said, as she updated the hologram to a miniature version of a spaceship.

"Great, we'll arrive soon. Get prepared," J'tan's glare found the two Undrians. "And make sure to keep it quiet and peaceful this time."

Evi's shoulders slumped. "But where's the fun in that?"

The beginning of an idea formed in my mind. *I might just have a way to prove myself after all.*

THE NEXT MORNING I went straight to cleaning the air ducts after a breakfast of Yul fruits. Tasting like pears and cinnamon, it was one of the exotic fruits I enjoyed, and I didn't have to worry about it making me sick.

None of us were sure exactly what food humans could eat from the surrounding planets. In order to find out, I was a human guinea pig. Every meal, Avi would hook me up to a health scanner. I'd take small bites, and he would watch my vitals, checking for any intestinal distress or poisoning. So far the worst food was meat from a type of crustacean found on the twin's planet,

Undri. I spent several hours in the bathroom after, forced to listen to Avi and Evi's snickers each time they checked on me. Lucky for me, the majority of the foods the crew stocked were safe for human consumption.

Unfortunately, safe didn't translate to tasty. The majority of the food was hard to choke down. Turned out, humans had much more delicate taste buds than the Undrians or Alderians, with most food being overpowering or extremely sour.

After another morning of food-roulette, I washed down the extremely bitter D'eleg vegetable with a glass of Yul juice. On my way out of the cafeteria, I grabbed my trusty bucket and rags and opened the doors to J'tan's workshop. Half-fixed machines and parts cluttered the tables and floors leaving little room to walk through. Not sure what anything was, I stepped carefully around each piece of machinery trying to reach the air duct. Halfway through removing the grate, J'tan entered the room, stopping when he saw me.

"We're going on a short mission, we should be back soon." He fished for something in one of the many pockets that lined his shimmery black pants and jacket.

I took note of the several knives strapped to his belts and two blasters that sat on each side. Apparently he did not trust the twins to keep this mission peaceful. Once he found what he was looking for, he handed me a small clear orb that glimmered green in the light. I held it gently, not entirely sure what to do with it.

"This is a communicator, I programmed it to reach any of us. If anything happens, just stay on the ship and call." His gaze was heavy.

"Yeah of course, I'll be right here." I smiled, hoping he couldn't see through my ruse.

He held my gaze, scrutinizing me. I picked up the buckets and rags and headed into the air duct. J'tan watched for a minute before turning to leave. My act worked. J'tan gave one final goodbye and left the room.

I set down my cleaning supplies and stilled my breath. Ear to the door, I waited till I heard the large exterior door of the ship close. After a moment of waiting to make sure they had left, I took off into the hallway. Rushing, I ran to the weapons room. I grabbed a large helmet and small blaster from a rack that housed a large assortment of weapons. I shoved the blaster in my jumpsuit and placed the helmet over my head.

You got this Val, just grab the cat-man and show them you aren't dead weight.

A dashboard appeared across my view. Unable to read anything, I smacked the helmet a couple times till it disappeared. *Old solutions for new problems.* Another thing I needed to learn.

Hopefully the alien characters weren't as difficult to read as they appeared.

Spotting a pair of handcuffs on a table, I grabbed them and shoved them into my jumpsuit pockets. As prepared as possible, I opened the ship's door.

Lush green greeted me on the other side. Bird songs and the smell of petrichor filled my senses. Staring up, it took me a second to comprehend what I was looking at. A band of white cut the cerulean sky in half. I was distracted from the strange sky as several green and red creatures, similar to birds without beaks, scattered from a tree above me. I took a couple steps down the ramp, looking at the distant blue beneath that was broken up by the massive trees sprawled across the land as far as the eye could see. *The Revenge* hovered over the canopy of branches leading to the ramps that spiraled around each large trunk. Each ramp led up to bridges that connected each tree to another. Various other ships were perched atop each tree, tethered by small ramps with colorful flags hanging beneath. Gliders zoomed to and fro, carrying aliens of all shapes and sizes. Each glider was driven by a small hairy alien with large ears and eyes, flying with expert precision, perfectly dodging the many branches and oncoming gliders.

Without the adrenaline that had followed me

through my last excursion through the space station, I was truly able to be in awe of my surroundings. *Abel would love it here.* Memories of being dragged to the newest sci-fi movies by my brother pulled at my heartstrings. Though he hadn't cut me off completely like my parents had after renouncing my religion, his only communication came in the form of a yearly Bible quote Christmas card.

I'd never wished for a camera more than at this moment. I tried to memorize every color, smell, and sight. I could only hope that I'd return home to share my tales. *They'll think I'm crazy.* I turned from my thoughts as I watched another group board a glider. J'tan, Avi, and Evi shuffled with the crowd boarding the small vessel. I took in one last glance at the stunning landscape around me, savoring as much as I could before taking off down the ramp.

I approached a crowd and got in line behind a rotund alien with several quills protruding from its red arms and back. Keeping my distance from the sharp looking quills, I inched my way forward as the queue continued to move steadily towards the line of gliders waiting for new passengers.

I watched as the quilled-alien in front of me placed his palm on a small orb that turned green with his touch. The driver seemed uninterested with his job, barely glancing at the orb as each passenger boarded. I kept as close to the alien in front of me as I could without getting stabbed, holding my breath—afraid that I might be caught. I passed the orb without touching it, and looked at the pilot. He made no indication that he had noticed, and I took a seat as far in the back as possible.

After the glider filled with passengers, we took off into the air. I was grateful for the helmet hiding my childish smile. The driver spoke as we passed more massive trees, his language unintelligible. The crowd *oohed* and *aahed* as we passed another tree, this one with golden leaves that glowed like fireflies. *Did the crew decide to go sight-seeing without me?*

As the driver narrated more about another glowing tree, this one red instead of gold, my helmet started beeping as more of the unreadable characters blocked my view. I smacked it several times, trying to stop whatever was going on. The large quilled alien looked at me quizzically, his large flat nose twitching as his solid black eyes focused on me. I gave the helmet another desperate hit and the beeping and characters finally disappeared. I breathed a sigh of relief once the alien's attention returned to the weird alive-Christmas trees.

The glider slowed, approaching a wide platform with a large spaceship docked upon it. The spaceship was lined with large windows, looking like the same one shown on Evi's hologram. I spotted the three familiar aliens boarding the ship. I kept them in my sights as the glider landed, making sure I blended with the crowd. It wasn't hard to follow them, as J'tans large frame stood above the many aliens. I kept low and followed the trio up the ramp and into the ship.

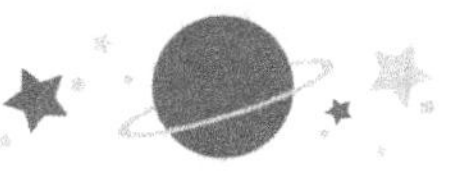

EIGHT

Star System 9

TE'RYN

A small child stared up at me, unmoving, her large gray eyes focused solely on me. I looked around for whoever might be in charge of her. I spotted her parents at the end of the room, distracted by the souvenir cart that had been pushed through the rows of the many travelers leaving the planet of Yoru. The cart held delicate candies spun into the famous landmarks of the planet. The choice was apparently a difficult one, as the parents continued to bombard the salesman with questions, ignoring their child completely.

Typical of cheaper shuttles, the seats sat close together squeezing a hundred or more passengers in the small viewing room. Unfortunately, I was one of those passengers. Stuck in between a family of Grismoths, I had to keep my arms folded to avoid being struck by their quills.

The child continued to watch me as she stuck a piece of candy to my pants. A wide smile stretched across her face. Not wanting to make a scene, I picked the candy from the fabric, flicking it across the aisle. She began to cry. Her mother's attention moved from the cart to my direction, searching for the cause. I quickly turned my head towards the clear panels surrounding the floor of the ship in an attempt to avoid unnecessary conflict.

The panels gave an excellent view of the rings of the green planet beneath us. Although I would have liked to, I was not here to sightsee. Merrick, a Jaxian scientist, was on the run after being caught working on highly illegal experiments. His benefactor decided he didn't want any loose strings and sent me to the ship Merrick was currently on—this overcrowded, cheap thing. The scientist had the bad luck of having me hired to take care of him, as I never missed my target.

As I watched the green planet shrink from view, I felt a stab of a quill as a Grismoth turned to talk to her partner. I pulled the quill out of my arm and jacket, flicking it at her as I walked away. Maybe it was Merrick's good luck that I was here to put him out of his misery. This shuttle was unbearable. I carefully shuffled my way through the tight space making sure to avoid any more mishaps to my clothing.

In the hall to the next floor stood a massive Alderian with a scar across his left cheek. Him and the two Undrians nearby carefully watched each passenger as they passed into the next viewing room. His hand rested on a blaster—not so discreetly hidden under his jacket.

Bounty hunters.

The Alderian's attention flicked to me for a moment then quickly moved on to the passenger behind me. I was not the only one looking for the scientist. I would have to be quick if I wanted to get him first. Keeping the bounty hunters in my peripheral, I waved my hand over the scanner, opening the doors to the next level. I instantly spotted Merrick. Seated near the viewing panels, his gray fur and long tail easily gave him away.

His head remained turned towards the panels, pretending to be mesmerized by the several icy moons the ship passed. Still conscious of his surroundings, Merrick's eyes darted back and forth watching the entering passengers. I kept my distance. I would have to lure him out of the crowd.

As I considered my options, I became distracted by a short figure with a large helmet wobbling with each step. They made their way towards the scientist, an outline of a blaster visible through a baggy black jumpsuit. *The bounty hunters are getting careless.* I noticed Merrick watching the helmeted figure cautiously, but he remained seated.

Waiting.

The bounty hunter stopped midway to watch the several large moons filling the view outside. Entranced, the hunter failed to see the scientist leave his seat. I stalked my way through the crowd following him. Finally noticing Merrick's absence, the bounty hunter searched around as if startled to see him missing even after the clumsy attempt to approach him. Eventually recapturing him in their sights, the bounty hunter took off after him, sending Merrick into a full sprint.

Vaat! Things just got more difficult. I cursed as I followed in pursuit.

When I turned the corner, the scientist had vanished. The hunter's helmet wobbled rapidly as they swung their head side to side frantically searching. I watched as Merrick emerged from the other side of the crowd near some paid thugs. Spotting him as well, the bounty hunter shifted their weight, preparing to chase after him.

"Not so fast," I grabbed the hunter by the neck of their jumpsuit. "What kind of bounty hunter are you?"

She let out a squeak of surprise. "Um, I..."

She stumbled over her words. The thugs turned their attention to us and I pulled her into a private viewing room. "Hold on. What are you doing? He's my target," she said as she fought against my grip, failing to do anything but wrinkle the old jumpsuit further.

"I'm not particularly in the mood to get caught in the middle of a shootout today. Ugh, this is why I hate kids, you can't even think first."

"I'm not a kid, I'm just new," she said, enunciating the vowels with a strange accent.

She looked smaller up close. She didn't have the four arms of the Azzeks nor the large ears of the Entari. Alderian didn't even seem to be her native language. My curiosity was piqued. "First of all, you're incredibly suspicious with this helmet on." I reached to remove it.

She grasped it tightly to her head. "I am suspicious without it, I have a lot of scars."

"Scars from what?"

"I got in this fight with this huge guy…"

I laughed, "Was it a *massaye*?" There was no way the domesticated grazing animal would do anything other than accidentally step on a foot. But I was in the mood to give this kid a hard time for almost messing up my mission.

"Yeah, and he had a lot of knives. Anyway, I took him down, so you don't want to mess with me." She strengthened her stance.

This is getting ridiculous. I snatched the helmet

off her. Her hands flew up trying to reach it. She was too slow. Green eyes met mine as I freed her head from the helmet. She was lovely. Escaped strands from the bun of brown hair haloed her oval face. Emotions clearly displayed in full force. Surprise, then irritation. "You're far from home, little human. What are you doing here?"

"Proving myself." She pulled her blaster out and pointed it in my direction. She let out a small gasp of pain as she maneuvered her right shoulder. *Far from home and injured.* I hadn't expected to ever run into a human again, especially not here of all places.

"And if you could be so kind as to return my helmet, I'll be on my way."

"Before you decide to point a blaster at someone, you should make sure it's charged first." I grabbed the blaster, dwarfing the small model in my hand. Her finger pulled the trigger. Nothing happened. Her expressive eyes switched from irritation to fear.

"Relax, if I wanted to hurt you, I would have let those thugs blast you apart." I released the gun.

The light from the aurora outside danced in her green eyes as they searched mine, looking for a lie. There was none, not this time. I was genuinely curious how a human had ended up here as a bounty hunter. Her appearance had turned this boring mission into something much more exciting.

"Look, you're clearly after this guy too. I'll give you half of the bounty if you help me," she said, a note of distress in her voice.

"Split it eighty-twenty, extra for teaching you how to use a blaster, and because I'll have to do more work since you're injured."

"Sixty-forty should be enough. I'm a quick learner, and it's just a little sore." She rolled her shoulder and gave me a sly smile, her pink lips turning up slightly.

I didn't consider myself easily persuaded, but when I saw that smile, it was over. "Deal." The contract didn't say *when* Merrick had to be killed after all.

She willingly handed me the blaster and I gave her a tutorial on how to charge each blast. True to her word, she was a quick learner. After being shown once, she was able to perfectly repeat the steps, successfully preparing the weapon.

"You know, where I'm from, it's polite to share names before you potentially die together."

I snorted at her comment. "If you get killed by those incompetent thugs than this isn't really the line of work you should be in."

"That wasn't what I was asking." Her cheeks reddened.

She was a cheeky little thing. I considered giving her one of my many aliases, but I wanted to hear my name from her mouth. "Te'ryn."

"Nice to meet you Te'ryn. I'm Val. So what's *your* plan?"

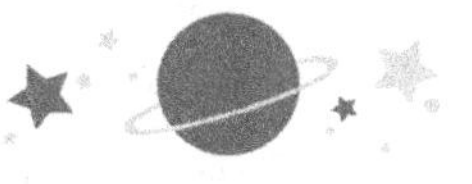

NINE

Star System 9

VAL

Should I trust the alien twice my size that knows I'm a human? Probably not. Do I have a better option at this point? Not really. I had snuck aboard this shuttle to capture the cat-man—Merrick, to prove I wasn't worthless. Maybe once we snagged him I could take Merrick away from Te'ryn and take all the credit. I considered my choices as I watched Te'ryn carefully. He was focused on the view outside, only his head poking through the sliding door.

"Coast is clear," he said as he pulled his head back into the room.

He was handsome. More than any human man I had ever seen. His gray Alderian skin was flawless, his cheek bones put models to shame, and his silver eyes seemed to glimmer in the light.

Is that why you trusted him so easily, because he's hot?

I shook my head subconsciously. Of course not, I had no idea how to use a blaster, I needed help. At least, that's what I told myself.

A smile crept across Te'ryn's face as he watched me with curious eyes. *Okay, it's definitely because he's hot.* His smile looked like it belonged to an angel. *Marie would be beside herself in happiness to see this alien.* I felt a pang of sadness remembering the women from the Azzek ship. I forced my thoughts back to the task at hand. Now was not the time to get distracted. Especially not with this handsome, yet suspicious Alderian in front of me. Te'ryn fiddled with a knife strapped to his thigh as he waited for me to give the signal to go.

Hopefully his intentions were good, because I might've just followed this Alderian into any sketchy spaceship. I slapped my face, reminding myself why I was here on this mission. Te'ryn returned the dagger to its sheath, then pushed his white hair from his eyes as they lit up in amusement. He said nothing about my weird face slapping. I needed to act less crazy around him. Or more—so he wouldn't even entertain the idea of kidnapping me.

"Ready?" I asked, cheeks slightly pink.

He gave a nod then set off through the door. I put my helmet back on and followed after him.

For his large size, he was surprisingly nimble. He slid through the crowd with ease. I scanned the crowd looking for the cat-man I had unfortunately scared off earlier. Merrick had disappeared once again. Lucky for us, he didn't have far to go. Te'ryn had assured me taking an escape pod would be the scientist's last resort as he was desperate to reach the planet the shuttle was heading towards.

Not wanting to seem like a complete rookie, I didn't ask what that planet was called. I couldn't read the swirling letters spelling out our destination either. I would really have to ask J'tan to teach me when—if—I got back. I steeled my nerves as I continued to follow Te'ryn.

I followed Te'ryn through the crowd till we reached another door. The door slid open after a touch to a nearby panel and we ascended the clear stairs to the next level. Vertigo hit as I looked down at the expanse of space clearly visible through the transparent steps. Te'ryn slowed, his eyebrows raised in question. I shook my head and continued on, keeping my eyes forward. After we passed through another door, I spotted our target.

Merrick sat in an empty room, his gaze heavy. "Rerris idd sillr va leeerrrr," he said, as two Alderians with blasters stepped beside him.

"What did he say?" I whispered to Te'ryn.

"You don't even have a translator?" He

flashed a surprised look. When I didn't answer, he continued. "He told us to drop our weapons if we want to live."

"How original. I could have guessed that." Being in space had made me more confident. Guess losing everything you love could do that to a girl.

Te'ryn laughed then raised his hands above his head. I followed suit, not sure what Te'ryn was thinking.

Merrick looked content with this development. He spoke to his bodyguards, sending them towards us.

"Please tell me this is part of your plan." I was starting to panic. I shouldn't have trusted him.

Te'ryn gave me a wink. Standing frozen in place, he waited till the bodyguards started to frisk him for weapons. In the blink of an eye, Te'ryn pulled one of the bodyguards forward, throwing him off balance. As the guard attempted to catch himself, Te'ryn plunged a black dagger into his throat causing him to fall backwards.

The other bodyguard jumped back in surprise, targeting her blaster on Te'ryn. I fumbled with the fabric of my jumpsuit, trying to free my own blaster. Just as I aimed at the bodyguard, another black dagger flew through the air catching her in the eye. She let out a scream. I couldn't help but gag. Seeing things on TV was one thing, in life, another thing entirely. *Okay, definitely not going to try and pull a fast one on this guy.* He could keep all the bounty if he wanted.

Merrick turned on his heel and ran, his long tail bouncing behind him. Te'ryn wasted no time in sending another dagger after him. It seemed impossible that the dagger would find its mark with such a far target. But Te'ryn did not disappoint as the dagger pinned Merrick's tail to the ground. Merrick yowled as he struggled to free his tail.

Te'ryn strode over to him, slow and confident. He said something in a language I couldn't understand. At those words, Merrick stopped struggling. I could swear I saw the last speckles of color leave Merrick's gray fur as he looked at Te'ryn in terror.

"Do you have any cuffs?" Te'ryn turned his attention back to me.

Grateful that was one thing I did think to bring, I handed them to him. My shaky hands nearly dropped them, but Te'ryn's quick reflexes caught the cuffs before they hit the floor. I had a long way to go as a bounty hunter, that was for sure. But I didn't think I would ever be able to kill as easily as Te'ryn. I tried my best to ignore the corpses on the ground. *They are just aliens,* I repeated to myself, but it didn't help the queasy feeling rising in my stomach. I watched as Te'ryn placed the cuffs around Merrick. He pulled his dagger free from Merrick's tail in a smooth motion. Wiping it clean on Merrick's clothes, he returned it to its sheath.

"If you swipe your palmpad over it, then you can control the cuffs," he explained as he waved over the cuffs, the light switching from red to blue.

"I don't have one of those either." I sighed, another helpful piece of technology I didn't own.

Te'ryn looked thoughtful for a moment. "How did you even become a bounty hunter anyway?" He pushed Merrick to his knees facing away from us.

"It's a long story."

His hand grabbed mine as he lifted the large helmet off my head. Noticing my glare, he returned it with a smile. "A gift in exchange for the tale."

He touched his ear, freeing the silver ring. I held completely still, not sure exactly what he wanted. I had trusted him but after seeing how dangerous he was, I was seriously doubting that choice more than ever. He placed the silver ring in my ear, stroking my face with a gentle hand before pulling away and replacing my helmet. The cool metal seemed to warm instantly, the foreign feeling disappearing. My eyes scanned

Te'ryn, looking for an explanation of what he had just done.

Please don't be a weird brain eating parasite.

When he gave none, I added it to my growing list of things to ask J'tan. I wasn't going to do anything to risk getting on Te'ryn's bad side.

Te'ryn waited for me to speak, completely ignoring the scene around him as if it was just another day on the job. I wasn't quite sure where to start with my story, and I didn't know if it was the smartest to give that information to a stranger like him anyway. Deep in thought of how to politely excuse myself, the doors to the room burst open. J'tan entered, blasters pointed at both of us as he spoke. "Hand the scientist over, he's our bounty."

"How unfortunate for you, we've seemed to capture him first," Te'ryn replied coolly, not taking his eyes off of me.

As J'tan took a cautious step forward, the doors opened again, revealing Evi and Avi. They stood still as two blasters were held to their heads by two larger Undrians dressed in black and yellow jumpsuits behind them.

"If you want them to live, hand over the scientist," the Undrian male on the right demanded.

"*Translating from Undrian,*" a voice pinged in my ear.

"You can shoot them, we don't care." Te'ryn stepped forward.

The Undrian pressed the blaster harder against Avi's head, his neck craning from the force. I placed my hand on Te'ryn's arm, stopping him.

"Never mind, I guess we do care," Te'ryn said, a hint of amusement in his voice.

He grabbed Merrick by the cuffs and threw him forward. The second Undrian stepped forward and grabbed him from the floor, pulling him towards the entrance. Sure that they had their bounty, the other Undrian sent Avi and Evi down to the floor with a kick.

"You twins put all Undrians to shame. *Weaklings.*" He spat and aimed the gun towards Avi's face.

His finger reached for the trigger, but Te'ryn was faster. He sent a black dagger sailing through the air, embedding itself into the Undrian's hand. The Undrian let out a scream and grabbed his hand, dropping his blaster.

"We had a deal, remember?" Te'ryn's voice turned poisonous, making the hair on the back of my neck stand.

A murderous glare crossed the injured Undrian's face but he followed the other as they exited the room, pulling Merrick behind them. A blast hit the door, sealing it as their last goodbye.

J'tan stared us down, confusion showing on his usually stoic face.

"We can't pay you if that's what you're looking for," J'tan broke the silence.

"Do you want them to pay? I'm sure I could convince him," Te'ryn whispered, his hand gripping another black dagger on his belt.

"No. They're my crew."

"Ah okay, well I guess this is a good place to part then. I can't let them get too far," he said, the irritation clear in his voice.

"Thank you." I looked up into his silver eyes.

"Till next time."

With one last wink he quickly exited the room through the opposite entrance. I wasn't sure why he had helped, but I was glad he did. I turned towards the three aliens in front of me and pulled off my helmet.

"Well, I didn't get the scientist, but I did save your asses. That should count for something." I felt a smile stretch across my face.

Avi's jaw dropped and Evi's eyes looked ready to burst.

"Val, what the *vaat* are you doing here?!" J'tan shouted.

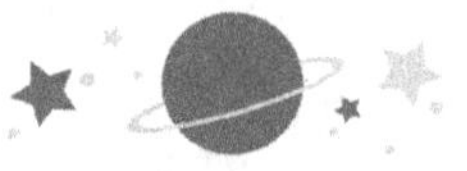

TEN

Star System 9

VAL

The group was silent as we took another shuttle back to the planet of Yoru. This shuttle was nearly empty compared to the packed one we had taken on the way over—to what I learned was an intergalactic space station. J'tan kept his eyes on me, no doubt rehearsing the lecture he would be giving as soon as we returned to *The Revenge*. Avi and Evi were unusually quiet. No argument nor teasing left their lips. I watched through the clear panels, captivated by the sight of asteroids and moons around us. I was certain it would be a long time before J'tan would let me off the ship again, so I spent my time enjoying the sights around me.

"You should have just let us die," Avi said, finally breaking the silence.

J'tan's eyes softened as he looked over at Avi. "You know I couldn't do that."

"If you did, you would have Merrick, you would have the money, and you wouldn't have to save our asses all the time." Avi's dark green hair fell in front of his intense yellow eyes and he pushed it out of the way. "And that idiot Aerix would still be alive," he said, standing.

Avi's words seemed to pierce J'tan. He swallowed and returned to staring out the windows. "You know he wouldn't want that."

Avi didn't stick around to hear J'tan's soft words. He stalked off through the set of doors leading to another level. I tried to catch Evi's eyes, curious what was going on, but her gaze was glued to the doors Avi had exited through. The uncomfortable silence continued the whole way back, the sour mood ruining the view.

Avi rejoined our group back at the ship, his quiet anger continuing. He pushed his way through the exterior door, heading straight for the cafeteria. J'tan met my eyes, giving me a look that said, *give him some time.* I gave J'tan a nod and headed towards the weapons room. After returning the helmet and blaster to their respective places, the doors slid open, Avi standing on the other side. I opened my mouth to speak but Avi cut me off completely. "I don't need a lecture from you of all people."

"Avi, I honestly don't understand what's going on." I held my hands up in a placating gesture. I didn't know who Aerix was or why the mention of his name made J'tan depressed and Avi so angry.

Avi's resentful gaze met mine. "No, of course you wouldn't, no weak creature from a developing planet would ever understand what it means to be born a twin in Undri."

"You don't need to be such a dick. I get you're angry but don't take it out on me."

He ignored me completely as he grabbed weapons from the racks, arming himself to the teeth.

Before I could share the choice words I had picked, Evi ran into the room, tackling Avi. "You think you can just *vaating* leave? Where will you go?" She screamed as she grabbed Avi's hair.

"Anywhere but here!" He yelled in response, grabbing Evi's hands. "I'm tired of being one of J'tan's pity projects." He pushed Evi away, knocking her and the weapons rack to the ground. I backed away, keeping my distance from the brawling aliens.

"This isn't what Aerix would want, you know he asked J'tan to take us in."

"Maybe he shouldn't have gotten killed so we wouldn't have to rely on his mate of all people."

At Avi's words, Evi barreled into him, knocking him against the wall near me. I shuffled towards the door, keeping track of the quarreling twins. Their fight knocked over another rack, causing more weapons to be strewn across the floor. I had almost made it to the door when Avi threw Evi off himself and on to me.

I felt something crack in my leg. The intense pain destroyed any shred of patience I had left. "Can you guys just fucking stop for a minute? What the fuck did I ever do to you?" I grabbed a blaster from the floor and aimed it at Avi.

He ignored me again, and charged at Evi—now standing ready for round two. I fired a blast hitting the wall behind him. The metal blackened from the impact of the blast, and Avi and Evi froze. J'tan crashed into the room, the metal doors squealing at the force he used to pry them open. He grabbed the two, pulling them apart.

"Evi. Out. Now!" J'tan's voice boomed as the twins struggled against his hold.

The twins stopped, continuing their argument with silent glares. Evi left the room first, leaving me and the other two behind.

"You too, Val," J'tan said, more gentle this time.

Pain radiated from my knee, and I was sure if I tried to stand, my leg would give out, but I didn't want to get caught in any more alien brawls. And despite it all, I still had some dignity left, albeit a small shred. I had lost everything. Stubborn as it was, I wasn't going to let that shred go as well. I gripped the wall and let out a hiss of pain as I attempted to stand with one leg. Realization dawned across J'tan's face, while guilt fell across Avi's. I felt tears trickle down my face as I struggled—and failed to stand.

"Just give me a minute." I slid to the ground. I thought I gained at least some respect after what had happened in the shuttle, but here I was showing how weak I was—again. *If there are any alien steroids out there, I'm going to take them all.*

"Avi! Fix this." J'tan pushed Avi forward.

I refused to meet his eyes. Two could play this asshole game.

"Sorry, Val," Avi said softly as he lifted me—without any effort.

Stupid aliens and their stupid superhero strength.

"He was my brother," Avi continued as he carried me gently to the med bay.

I stayed silent the whole time. I was in too much pain to object or ask questions. Avi set me gently on the metal table and pulled a small screen out—scanning me. "Vaat, Val why didn't you say anything about your shoulder?"

"I'm not exactly welcome here, and I had to work my share, remember?" The pain brought smart-mouth Val back. "Just wrap it up and I'll be okay in a little bit."

"Is that what they do on your planet? How inconvenient." He paused, "I am sorry you got caught up in our fight. Evi is better at expressing her emotions through her fists," Avi said, as he injected a clear blue liquid into my shoulder and knee.

I felt a burning sensation in each spot, the feeling quickly subsiding along with the pain. "Yeah, this is way better than waiting for it to heal."

I sat up from the table. My anger vanished along with the pain. I was almost ready to forgive Avi, *almost*. I watched curiously as Avi returned the syringes to the small drawer protruding from the white wall. "What happened to your brother?"

He sighed as he turned to face me. "He got killed on a mission. Evi and I overestimated our strength and tried to take on an entire crew. Aerix got us out, but only at the cost of his life."

"I'm sorry."

"Me too." He sat next to me, the small table bowing slightly beneath his weight. "You know, he's the reason we can understand you. He made us download your language after he found a crew of Azzeks that were heading to your planet. He was heroic like that, always wanting to help those weaker than him."

"I wish I could have met him." I was grateful for the Undrian I would never be able to meet. Without him I would've never had the chance to learn as much as I did from J'tan.

"He would have liked you. He liked cute and

tiny things." Avi smirked as I gave his shoulder a weak punch at his comment. "On Undri they usually kill twins when they are born. We aren't born as strong as the typical Undrian. It's shameful to have such weak family members. Our parents felt the same, but Aerix left his prestigious royal guard post to raise us. We were weak, sickly and useless but he still tried his best at bounty hunting to make enough to feed us."

"You know, I know a thing or two about being weak and useless," I chimed in.

Avi chuckled in response and continued. "That's how Aerix met J'tan, they met on a mission and hit it off instantly. J'tan had no problem taking in his mate's weak siblings, but Evi and I had to prove our worth."

"Sounds familiar." I let out a small laugh. Seemed we had more in common than we thought.

"I'm just so angry you know? Why would he give up everything for us—for me? If I wasn't born, everyone would be much better off."

"I'm sure no one feels that way, Avi," My chest constricted as I remembered feeling the same after I couldn't pray the gay away and I wanted nothing more than to never be born, that way I wouldn't feel like such a disappointment to my parents.

"Yeah, well, from one weakling to another, I

think you're stronger than you know." Avi returned to cleaning up the rest of the room.

"You too. And for what it's worth, I'm glad you're around, weakness and all."

Avi responded to my words with a warm smile. Feeling like it was best to give him some space, I left the room, stopping as I spotted Evi leaning against the wall near the medbay's door. Her gaze met mine and she mouthed a silent *thank you*.

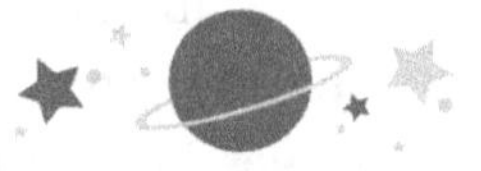

ELEVEN

Star System 26

VAL

1 year later

"**P**ull up, Val!" Avi shouted through the ship's communication system as I navigated the cruiser through an asteroid field.

"Good, now turn the ship right, and go through those two asteroids."

I gripped the cruiser's yoke forcing it to veer right, zooming in between the two asteroids. I kept my breathing even as I sent the ship forward, leaving only inches of clearance on each side. After making it through, I pulled the ship's yoke hard, spinning it back towards the main ship—*The Revenge.*

"That's my girl!" Avi said, a touch of pride in his voice.

"Great job, now head on back," I heard Evi say in the background.

I focused back on the controls and pulled into *The Revenge's* docking bay. The sister-brother twins greeted me as soon as I exited the ship.

"I knew you could do it! J'tan said you weren't ready but we proved him wrong didn't we?" Avi gave me a pat on the back.

J'tan entered the bay and gave a grunt of approval. *I'll take that as a job well done.* I had to claim my victories, no matter how small with J'tan. As captain, he was expected to run a tight ship. He required that each person of the team follow the plan down to the smallest detail. And I had gone slightly off course with my flying test. I just hoped he wouldn't give me too much of a difficult time over it. After my first attempt at bounty hunting, J'tan was adamant that I never do it again until he decided I was ready. His excuse being, *"I won't send a tiny human off to die."*

That stung my ego a bit, but I couldn't argue. I only partly-succeeded on my first 'mission,' because of the mysterious bounty hunter Te'ryn. I had asked the crew about him, but none of them could seem to find any information on him. Evi even traced the pass he used to board the shuttle but it was a fake. He was practically a ghost.

My attempt at bounty hunting wasn't in vain though, my first try at a mission had successfully convinced the crew there was a possibility I could be a bounty hunter. The past year, the crew had pitched in to help me train. They taught me how to shoot, fight and fly. The more I trained with them, the more the massive gap in our abilities became clear. J'tan had asked me to earn my share, but with how new to this I was, it was clear I wouldn't be able to contribute much.

After we left the docking bay, we all convened around a table in the cafeteria. Evi sat sipping on her fifth cup of Conag for the day—a sour caffeinated drink. And Avi filled the silence prattling on about his next vacation destination while J'tan worked on a small screen. As soon as J'tan opened his mouth to speak, Avi shut his.

"I picked up a new contract. This one's a quack doctor. I sent the necessary information to all of you." His gaze turned to me.

"Wait, me?" I looked at all my crewmates, waiting for the punchline.

"No, the parasite inside you, Val," Avi pointed to my stomach.

Evi punched his arm. "You've done a great job so far, Val. You're ready." She gave me a warm smile.

"Don't tell me you've already given up on returning to Earth?" J'tan's eyebrow quirked.

Of course I hadn't given up. Getting home was a much more difficult task than I would've ever thought. I'd already been stuck here for a year because getting back to Earth was an expensive endeavor. First I would have to find a crew willing to make the highly-illegal trip. Then that crew would need to have a large enough ship that could make the long journey—those were far and few between. Not to mention the trip would cost hundreds of thousands of credits.

While I didn't need to worry about paying for food and board by helping with necessary maintenance on the ship, I didn't have an opportunity to make money either. This job was the real first step towards getting home. I swallowed down my nervousness, forcing a smile on my face. "You can count on me!"

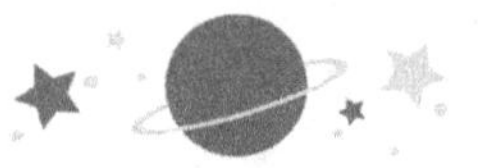

TWELVE

Star System 27

TE'RYN

T he bouncer scanned my pass with a slow pace that would put Undrian mollusks to shame.

"Everything looks to be in order," he said, looking up from his tablet.

"I sure hope so. I paid an obscene amount of credits for those." I flashed him a smile.

His face remained stone cold.

"It was a joke, no need to be so serious." I gave his muscular arm a pat as I walked through the now open door.

Club Eclipse was barely a step above the seedy bars I met most of my clients in. While there were no active fights going on, or panels falling from the ceiling, the club still smelt of silversalt smoke and sweaty bodies.

I continued through the hallway, stopping before the doors. Making sure my face was disguised, I entered the room. I made an error on a previous job, forcing me to keep up the façade of Dr. Fet'lan till my contact could erase the image of my face from every database.

I scanned the room for the bar. Spotting it, I pushed my way through the crowd. Flashing lights painted the room various colors while dancers of all races entertained on raised platforms. A dancer's gaze followed me through the crowd. She waved her hand, gesturing to me to join her on the pedestal. I shook my head and continued on my path.

I remembered the scars too well to make that mistake again. I instinctively ran my thumb along the large scar on the back of my hand. When I was young and cocky I had gotten involved with a gorgeous dancer. Turned out the cost was more than I could pay, and I was used as an example of what happened when you couldn't afford the exorbitant fees the club owner charged.

I shook the bad memories aside; I wouldn't stay here long. Eventually I made it to the bar— only after my boots had been thoroughly trampled by the many intoxicated patrons. It was part of my routine. Get a drink, get information, then get out.

I tapped the screen pulling up my favorite Korop brand.

"Sixteen credits? Yeah, no," I muttered under my breath as I turned away from the bar.

I scanned the second floor looking for the yellow lit booth. Once in my sights, I returned to the crowd. Hopefully part two of the routine turned out better than part one. Reaching the booth, I knocked six times—the code this particular client had picked.

Much easier than saying a stupid phrase. I was already starting to like this client.

"Enter," called a voice from inside the room.

I stepped in, heat blasting my face. I took note of my client. A large Basillian sat sipping a drink, observing the crowd below. I unzipped my jacket and sat down. The Basillian set down its glass, yellow light glinting off its slick textured green skin.

"I've heard you're good at what you do." Its large black bulging eyes locked on mine.

"So I've been told." I leaned back, arms draped on the couch and resting my ankle on my knee. *Two can play at this dominance game.*

The Basillian took another sip of its drink. "I have *information.* Information on an object that could lead to this being the last job you'll ever need."

I leaned in, keeping my curiosity off my face. "An object? Not my typical line of work."

"I'm aware this is out of your *expertise,* but your skill of going unseen is what I need."

"I'll hear you out at least." I poured myself a glass, raising it to the Basillian, then downing it in one swig. *Aged Grecco, this client has expensive tastes.*

"A crown jewel is going to be transported across Star System Seventy-Three for the coronation of the new emperor. The *Heart of the Renari.* It can go on the market for at least forty-million credits." The Basillian tapped its tapered fingers on the glass.

"Through Star System Seventy-Three? That's a risky move for such a precious jewel."

"The Renari are not currently on good terms with the Federation after the death of a crown prince in their territory."

"Ah." I took another sip of my drink.

"I have the schedule for the ship. All you'll need to do is slip in, grab the jewel, and slip out without anyone knowing the wiser. If you bring the jewel to me, I'll give you twenty-million for your work."

"Half? Why so generous?"

The Basillian poured itself another drink. "I can assure you that no one else will be as generous as me."

He wants to make sure I don't find another buyer. I swirled my drink, taking a moment to think. "You've got a deal."

"It will be a pleasure working with you." It flashed a toothy grin.

Exiting the booth with the Renari's schedule and ship blueprints, I made my way back to the bar. I ordered two glasses of Korop, celebrating the large sum I was about to earn.

"I hope it's not a female that's got you so happy." I turned and saw an Alderian female leaning on the counter next to me. Her long black hair draped over a shimmering dress that wrapped around her toned body. The colors of the dress switched with each flash of the lights.

"And why is that?" I asked.

"Because I was going to ask if you could buy me a drink."

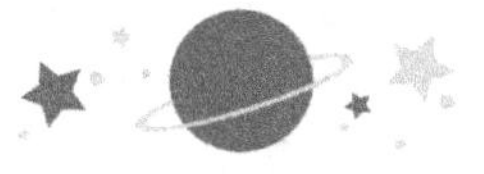

THIRTEEN

Star System 27

VAL

I rubbed my sore shoulders as I made my way through the crowded street towards Club Eclipse. J'tan had been especially tough with the last training session. He made me repeat my grapples and throws for what felt like hours till he was happy with my technique. He was concerned about sending me on my first mission and wanted me prepared, though it might have been for nothing, as I could barely lift my arms without my muscles screaming in protest. Not paying attention, I let out a gasp as I almost collided with an Undrian dressed in a nearly see-through suit. She shot me a nasty look and I muttered an apology and picked up my pace.

For my disguise, Avi and Evi had me dress in chunky spiraled heels, a short dress, and enough blue paint to cover the ship—their attempt to make me look less human and more Undrian.

Though, even with heels I could barely match their height.

"Remind me why I, the only human on this side of the galaxy, has to avoid notice and follow the target?" I asked, fixing my dark green wig.

"Because the last time we were there, Avi got us permanently banned," Evi replied through my earpiece communicator.

"Maybe they were just jealous that I so easily upstaged the dancers," Avi muttered.

"And what if someone asks why I'm half the height of an Undrian?" I stepped around a Jaxian couple who walked side-by-side with tails intertwined.

"Our disguise is perfect, no one will be able to tell," Avi said.

"Also if anyone asks why you're so short, just punch them!" Evi added unhelpfully.

I'm sure that would go over well.

"Focus," J'tan said, and the twins quieted.

The plan was simple. I was to locate the quack doctor in the club, follow him *discreetly*, then place a tracker on his ship. After I did my part, the rest of the crew would follow and apprehend him while he was alone in space, finally finishing the job by turning him into the proper authorities. I was to meet up with them afterwards to split the bounty.

Luck was on our side as we happened to be in the same star system when the target was spotted heading into Club Eclipse. We were able to make our way over quickly to Tratan, a small ocean planet filled with floating cities. I took my time enjoying the fresh air. I'd been trapped on the ship for so long I forgot what it felt like to breathe air that hadn't run through a filter millions of times. The only thing that would make this trip outside better, was the sun. It had been over a year since I'd been in light that wasn't artificial, though the six moons hanging in the sky were pretty enough to make up for it. Tratan was best known for its nightlife, all races convened here looking for ways to blow off steam.

I continued my path through the bustling streets, making my way to the back of the line for entry to the club. Ahead of me stood two short Jaxians covered in striped fur with several piercings running down their cat-shaped ears, talking excitedly.

"Oh, I hope the bouncer lets us in this time," one of the Jaxians said in her growl-like language.

"Don't worry, my cousin said these passes are legit," the other Jaxian confidently replied.

My translator perfectly interpreted the alien language into English. Te'ryn had given me an expensive model, one with thousands of languages downloaded. The crew was suspicious of why he would so easily part with such an expensive piece of technology. After several scans, Evi returned it to me, declaring it had no trackers or anything of concern. That made me even more confused why Te'ryn had gifted it to me. We hadn't seen or heard anything of the Alderian since our encounter on the Yoru shuttle. Luckily, the crew had finally equipped me with a palmpad as well, all pitching in to pay the costly hush fee to have a doctor install it in my hand.

Jaxians are a feline race that are known for their loyalty as well as their razor sharp claws, or cat-people as I liked to call them. I internally repeated the facts that the crew had forced me to study till I could name each species in my sleep.

The line moved quickly. Soon the females in front of me held out their passes to the towering bouncer. He scanned them, taking his time to study every word.

"Get outta here," his voice boomed.

"But-but these are legit!" One of the Jaxians squeaked.

The bouncer leaned down, eyeing the Jaxian. "You sure about that?"

The Jaxians took off down the street disappearing into the crowd. *Guess they weren't sure.*

The bouncer turned to me, hand held out. "Next!"

I swallowed and handed him my pass.

"You're pretty short for an Undrian," he said, scanning my pass.

"Punch him!" Evi said in my ear.

"No way!" I whispered back.

"What was that?" The bouncer turned his attention back to me.

"Oh- what- I mean no way, I hear that all the time!" I forced out a laugh.

"Hmm," was all he said as he handed back my pass. Evi's counterfeit had worked. He opened the door, gesturing inside. My "thank you" was drowned out by the blaring music escaping through the entrance. I wasn't a fan of alien music. It was too high pitched. Most of the singing sounded like an all soprano opera performing in a room filled with only helium.

"Oh lucky you, Val, it's your favorite music," Avi chimed in.

Avi and Evi teased me mercilessly about my "uncultured ears." Whenever they had the chance, they would play as much of their music as possible around me. I was a pro at tuning it out. Luckily, this music was mostly covered up by loud beats, making it more bearable.

A pang of nostalgia hit me as I watched the dancing crowd. *Steph would love it here.* Last time my best friend and I went out clubbing we ended up drunk on the public library's lawn with two and a half extra pairs of shoes. Steph kept the shoes, claiming that they were memories and we couldn't just throw them away. I let out a small laugh as I recalled how long she kept the things. *I'll be back soon, Steph.*

I stumbled through the crowd, cursing my too-tall heels.

"Now Val, we won't judge if you find a male or female you want to spend some alone time with," Avi said as a massive Alderian knocked into me, almost sending me flying across the floor.

"I'm not here to fuck!" I said.

The Alderian glanced at me and I quickly averted my gaze, squeezing myself farther into the crowd.

"Avi, she's tiny," Evi replied, "any male here would rip her in ha-"

I turned off my earpiece.

Focused on finding a good vantage point, I scanned the club. Naked dancers set high above the crowd on pedestals swayed with each beat of the music. Intricate patterns snaked across their bodies changing with each flash of the lights. It was mesmerizing, but I couldn't afford to get distracted. I forced myself to look for the target.

From where I was, the only thing I could see were the backs of all the aliens around me. *Why are aliens so tall?* Spotting a bar counter on a raised platform, I slowly pushed my way through the crowd.

I pulled myself up onto a stool, feeling like a

child with my legs dangling above the step. At five-foot-seven, I never felt short back on Earth, but being surrounded by tall aliens did change your perspective a bit. I turned my earpiece back on, pretending to brush my hair back as I scanned the room.

"Any sign of the target?" J'tan asked.

"Nada."

"Val, no human words, you're undercover."

"Sorry," I said quietly, turning to look at the bar menu. The bar was staffed by robot arms, serving the large crowd quickly and with expert precision. I swiped through the menu built into the glass looking for the few liquids I knew wouldn't cause intestinal distress. I clicked the order on a glass of Korop and scanned my hand transferring the appropriate amount of credits. I would never get used to the metal implanted under the skin of my palm. I rubbed my hand subconsciously as the robot arm set down the glass in front of me.

"Korop, good choice, good choice," Avi said, as I took a sip and winced.

Just like straight tequila. A conversation to my right caught my attention and I subtly turned, taking in the faces of the speakers.

An Alderian male with white hair, a prominent nose, and lines around his eyes sat one stool over.

It was the target, the quack doctor Fet'lan.

He was handsome, but still couldn't hold a flame to Te'ryn. *Stop thinking about him*, I scolded myself. I had one mission, and that was to get back to Earth. I couldn't get distracted.

Fet'lan continued to converse with a beautiful Alderian female with long black hair and a color changing strappy dress that criss-crossed around her body, accentuating all her toned muscles.

"It must be exciting being a traveling doctor," she cooed.

"It's not as exciting as it sounds." His silver eyes gleamed as he flashed a smile.

I swiveled back towards my drink taking a minute to calm myself. I needed to make sure he didn't notice me.

"Well, I'd better be off. I can't leave my patients waiting," he said, standing.

The female wrapped her arms around his toned biceps. "I'm sure they can wait a little bit, after all, doctors need breaks too right?"

"Not this one," he said, gently unwrapping her arms.

"She clearly can't take a hint," Avi murmured.

I let out a snort, quickly covering my mouth. Fet'lan's eyes snapped over to me. I looked back at my drink as if it held the secrets to the universe.

"Ahh Tyr, I was wondering when you would

show up." I felt Fet'lan's hand press on my upper back.

Certain my eyebrows had flown off my face entirely, I looked up at him, my mouth agape.

"Let's get out of here, shall we?" He asked with a wink.

If my brain was a computer I'm sure there would be a blue screen of death right now. Not only had I been noticed by the target, but he was now escorting me out of the club with his hand on my waist.

"Thanks for the save. She was going to drain me of all my credits," he said into my ear, hot breath brushing my face.

"Uh, sure, no problem." I forced my eyes to the ground avoiding his gaze. I felt the cool night air hit my face as we exited the club.

"Val. Status. Now!" J'tans voice blared in my ear. I kept my face straight, fighting back a wince.

"You're rather short for an Undrian." Fet'lan put his hand lightly on top of my head. "It's rather cute actually," he continued, his lips forming into an award-winning smile.

Mind blank, I felt my hand form into a fist, throwing a weak punch to his chest. His eyebrow quirked.

"Sorry, my—my sister told me to do that if anyone said I was short."

He let out a low laugh. *Space Jesus help me.* I

had just punched the target. J'tan would never let me go on a mission again.

"Sounds like you have a good sister. Thanks again for the help," he said, running a strand of my wig hair through his fingers.

I gave him a small nod. He flashed me one last smile and walked off melting into the crowd.

"Good job!" Evi said, snapping my mind back to the mission. I looked around, spotting Fet'lan's white hair bobbing in the crowd.

"Tracking the target now," I whispered as I popped out my yellow contact, replacing it with a clear one set with a small camera.

Half the height, I had to jog to keep up with the tall Alderian. He kept a steady pace towards the docks—positioned away from the club over the dark emerald ocean.

"We have sight, keep following the target," J'tan said.

I slowed my pace and kept myself hidden behind crowds, watching Fet'lan from a safe distance. He approached a ship surrounded by yellow glowing panels. Cursing, he tried to force the panels apart to no avail. Running his hand through his hair, he headed towards the dock attendant.

"Great work team," I said, making my way towards the ship.

"That wasn't us, just his bad parking job,"

Evi said. I chuckled as Fet'lan argued loudly over the cost with the attendant.

Now near the ship, I pulled the tracker from a small pocket in my dress. Twisting the half orb to activate it, I leaned forward to attach it underneath the wing.

"Hold on, that's a Spearrunner 4577-6," Avi interrupted.

"Translation please," I sighed, hand still in position.

"Oh sorry, let me translate to Stone Age. Ship go very fast. Tracker no stick."

"Maybe Blue Man should give better tracker." I rolled my eyes.

"Evi, can I get your help opening the door so I can place it inside?" I asked as I placed my hand over the door panel.

"Just a moment," she replied. After a couple seconds the door beeped and slid open. I took a breath and stepped inside the dark ship.

"Where should I put it?" I whispered.

"Anywhere he won't look any time soon," J'tan said.

I made my way down the hall, opening each door till I found the supply room. Stepping in, the room lit up. The small room held several metal crates scattered across the floor. Several guns hung along the walls. On the adjacent wall, black daggers that glinted in the light were all lined up, organized by size.

"Vaat, that's nothing a doctor would have, quack or not," Avi said softly.

"Get out of there now, Val!" J'tan exclaimed, his voice cutting out.

I turned to leave the room, stopping as I heard the sound of the exterior door opening.

"Dangerous. Whatever. Don't. Caught. Find you." J'tan's transmission was filled with static.

"Guys, this isn't funny. Come on. Hello?" I asked, receiving only silence in return.

Star System 79

TE'RYN

*C*urse *this planet and its awful clubs, leeching females, and ridiculous parking laws.* Nothing I had said could convince the attendant to lower the fine. That attendant was lucky. If I hadn't been in a hurry he would have sung a different tune entirely. I let out a sigh, falling back into the pilot seat. The only good thing that had come out of this trip was the once in a lifetime contract. *And the cute Undrian.* I smiled as I remembered how every emotion had shown on her face. She reminded me of Val. Berries and spice, that's what the tiny Undrian had smelled of, exactly like the small human. I was curious what Val was up to, how far she'd made it as a bounty hunter, but I'd never had the chance to run into her again.

I would have preferred to buy drinks for Val, or the Undrian, rather than the female that intended to have me spend every last credit to my name.

I pulled up the plans of the Renari ship. Hundreds of levels populated on the hologram —each room, cannon and escape pod shown down to the smallest detail. The ship was heavily armed. I'd expected that, but I didn't expect it to be armed with the latest Alderian technology. That would complicate matters. My home planet was well known for its superior weapons and technology. The stealth on my ship would be useless against it. Getting near the carrier would be more difficult than I anticipated. With only five rotations before the Renari carrier passed through Star System Seventy-Three, I had very little time to prepare. Despite that, the credits were incentive enough; I cracked my knuckles and started to piece together a plan.

I spent the next couple days cooped up in my room, only leaving for bathroom and food breaks. I needed every second I could get to formulate a plan. I figured I could make it close to the carrier, but if I left my ship to enter and retrieve the *Heart of the Renari*, my ship would be destroyed by the many patrolling sentries, leaving me trapped. Working solo made this mission nearly impossible.

After another failed attempt at a plan, I groaned and threw my blanket off. *Maybe I should just turn this contract down.* Heading towards the food bay, I heard a soft *thump* from inside. I silently retraced my steps, returning to my room. I armed myself with the several daggers I kept nearby and pulled a helmet over my head. The intruder was either very confident, or very dumb to stow away on my ship.

Stepping lightly, I tapped the panel opening the door. Reaching to my thigh, I pulled my dagger silently from its sheath. I positioned my arm ready to strike as the door slid open. Inside sat the tiny Undrian. Her one yellow and one green eye widened with surprise when she saw me. In her hand she held *my* food. The rest was stuffed into her mouth, causing her cheeks to swell.

"I guess I must have left a great impression for you to follow me all the way here," I said calmly, testing the sharpness of my dagger on my fingertip.

"I, uh. Ack," she coughed.

I threw the dagger. It skimmed her face before lodging in the wall behind her. She gulped as a red droplet of blood slid down her face. *Red?* Undrians had blue blood. I knew that because I had spent hours trying to get the deep cerulean stuff out of my nice jacket.

The not-Undrian pulled a dagger out of the top of her dress and threw it at me. I dodged it, pacing towards her. Throwing herself off the table and out of my line of sight, she flung another dagger in my direction. Catching it midair, I turned back to her. "Who sent you?"

"Yur unda awest fer quackery," she said, her words jumbled by the food in her mouth.

"Quackery?" My eyebrow twitched. *Is she on silversalt?*

She swallowed the rest of her food then spoke again. "Your days of bad medicine are over."

I laughed. *A bounty hunter, great.* I knew my doctor alias was growing old, but I thought it'd last at least a few more cycles.

I pushed the table to the side, cornering the small figure. "Look, if you're trying to seduce me in order to get me to turn myself in, you're going to have to try a lot harder."

She ran towards me, dropping to her knees as I reached out to grab her. My hand missed its mark as she slid in between my legs, popping up behind me. Before I could turn, she sent a swift kick to the back of my knee, forcing one leg down. *Not bad.*

"I'm not here to seduce you, I'm here to fight!" She snapped.

Before she could get away, my hand wrapped around her ankle pulling her down to the ground. With one hand, I pinned her arms above her head. I leaned down, locking eyes with her.

"You should try seducing, it might get you

further." She squirmed underneath my grip. It was no use, she was clearly outmatched.

"Short and weak, you're really not a typical Undrian."

One strap on her short silver dress had snapped, causing one side to dip, revealing a patch of pink skin just above the falling neckline. I ran my finger along the patch, feeling the difference between the smooth pink and the dry blue. A small shiver shook her body beneath my touch.

"Oh? Not an Undrian are we?" My eyes traveled back up, taking in her different colored eyes.

"That is none of your business!" She exclaimed, kicking her free leg towards my crotch.

I caught her foot mid kick. "Sorry darling, but I'm not really into foot-stuff," I said, stroking my thumb along the bottom of her bare foot.

"Are you sure? You don't want to try it out at least once?" She smiled, showing her white teeth.

Stars, she's gorgeous. And that smile seemed familiar.

"I'm willing to try a lot of things with you *darling*, but I'll need my equipment in good working condition."

She pursed her lips, emphasizing her round cheeks. Obviously thinking about her next move, her eyes darted around the room. Deciding to test my theory, I picked her up and threw her over my shoulder.

"Hey! Put me down!" She shouted, pounding on my back with her tiny fists.

"Can you move to the right? I'm a little tight there," I laughed. She let out a huff and stopped. I walked down the hallway towards the bathroom.

"Don't you try anything, my crew will be here any minute," she said, a slight tremble in her voice.

"Oh, don't worry about them disturbing us, I have a scrambler installed. Nothing gets in or out unless I want it to." I patted her leg.

I felt her heartbeat quicken as we entered the bathroom. I set her down in the shower as gently as one could set a wriggly, angry female and punched the water button.

The water streamed over her, washing the blue off her skin. The wet material left little to the imagination. Her nipples pebbled under the cold water, and the dress clung to every curve. A couple locks of brown hair fell beneath the green. I reached, pushing aside her defensive hands, and pulled the wig off her head. "How's bounty hunting going for you, Val?"

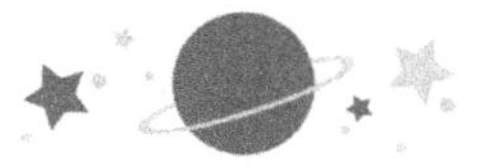

FIFTEEN

Star System 78

VAL

I *am such an idiot.* My teeth chattered as the cold water poured over me. I got overly confident about his routine and became careless. Now I was stuck in a shower with an overly strong, cocky alien. My mind raced thinking of ways to escape when the mention of my name snapped me back to the present. My eyes widened and my face paled. He knew who and what I was.

It had taken several glasses of Korop and other drinks to get J'tan to open up about what he knew about the fates of the other human women. It wasn't great. Alderian males quickly became obsessed with humans. Something about our features, scent, and curvier bodies enthralled them. Humans were considered novelties and were kept on the planet Grihan, serving only the wealthy and prominent males of the galaxies. While I was grateful I was able to get away, I couldn't shake the guilt for leaving the other women behind. When feeling particularly down, Evi and Avi would attempt to comfort me, telling me there was nothing I could have done against a crew of Azzeks. But I couldn't help but think about what could have been.

The large Alderian stood and turned the temperature of the water up.

"Clean up before you get blue stuff everywhere. We'll talk after," he said, leaving the bathroom. "And don't try anything funny, I'll cut off an appendage for each thing you break."

I decided to take advantage of his small mercy. *I haven't showered for days, at least I'll die clean.* I dropped my heavy dress to the ground with a *clank.* Evi had sewn as many knives as possible into the small dress, but it had given me blisters in all kinds of wrong places. I scrubbed my body, watching as the water turned from blue to clear. Calling it good, I shut off the water and activated the air jets. I left the shower and snooped around the bathroom.

"There's a robe on the shelf below," the Alderian said through the door. Not wanting to push my luck, I threw on the oversized robe.

"Ah much better, now I won't have to worry about cleaning blue paint off of everything." He smiled.

Gesturing for me to walk in front of him, I was ushered to the food bay. "Now if you don't mind, you can explain while I eat. I skipped my last couple meals and I'm absolutely ravenous."

He winked, pushing my shoulders down till I sat at the table. I took in a breath, not sure what to say. "So I take it you're not a doctor?" I cringed. Of all things to say, that's what came out?

"And what makes you think that?" He asked, filling his bowl from the dispenser.

"Well, for one, most doctors don't carry enough weapons to arm a small army." *God stop talking.* I scolded myself. He let out another low laugh. With how many times I'd made this Alderian laugh in the past hour, you'd think I was a comedian.

"No, I'm not a doctor. But you knew that already, Val." He tapped a button on his helmet and it collapsed into itself, revealing Te'ryn's face underneath. He was unfazed by the change as he focused on rubbing a smudge of blue paint off the table.

"Is Te'ryn even your real name?" I questioned. He finished his food and dumped the bowl into the cleaning shoot.

"Does it matter?" He handed me a glass of Kwik juice. I hated the bitter stuff, but I took the glass in my hands, keeping it on the table. He quirked an eyebrow, then took back the glass and downed the liquid in one gulp. "Hmm I thought you'd like that. What do you normally drink?"

"Does it matter?"

"No I guess, it doesn't. You already helped yourself to *my* food anyways," he said, filling the glass with a different liquid. He set down the glass in front of me, now filled with Yul juice. I took a small sip. "I figured you'd like that one. Humans have the taste buds of children." He looked at me, satisfied with his drink choice.

"Maybe Alderians don't have any taste buds," I mumbled into my drink.

He let out a laugh and returned to the table. "So, you were saying how you became a bounty hunter. I never got to hear that story."

I explained my capture, attempted escape, how I learned the Alderian language, then my actual escape. Just before telling him how I had blown the Azzek ship open, I stopped, slapping my hand on the table.

"Wait, weren't you just trying to kill me earlier? Why am I telling you this?" I inspected my drink, looking for an excuse for my loose lips. *If he thinks that giving me a shower and food will get me to talk, he's wrong.*

"Darling, I didn't *try* to kill you, if I had, you'd already be dead. And I wasn't the only one throwing knives. Anyway, don't stop now, you're getting to the good part." He flashed his dazzling smile.

Apparently that was all it took for me. *Space Jesus help me!* It was getting increasingly more difficult to keep up my guard around him. I continued the story. Te'ryn lost it at the part explaining how I blew up the Azzek's ship.

"That was you?!" He held his stomach laughing. "I can't believe- ha!" He wiped a tear from his eye.

I eventually finished the rest of the story, leading up to the present day. "Now, did my tragic story convince you to turn yourself in?" I grinned.

"No, but I'm still curious why your team let you join another mission when you're so vulnerable." He gestured to all of me.

"Hey! I might be small..." I paused. "And weak..." Pause. "But only compared to you aliens. I'm one hell of a pilot, so don't act like I'm completely useless." I chugged my drink then crossed my arms.

"A pilot huh?" Te'ryn said, taking my drink and refilling it. "I think that we can come to a compromise, little human." He reached out and grabbed my hand, his silver eyes gleaming.

SIXTEEN

Star System 73

TE'RYN

The universe must have heard my pleas, because the solution to my problem had walked on to my ship herself. Val was a pilot. *She also smells amazing.* Not that it would help with the mission, it was just a plus at this point. I stood up from the table, pulling Val behind me, her small hand held in mine. We walked towards the ship's bridge.

"Uh, want to tell me what you're doing?" She asked, trying to free her hand.

"You're a pilot right?" I held her hand tighter. We entered the bridge and I sat her down in the captain's chair. "Prove it." I sat in the co-pilot's chair.

"You're going to just let me fly your ship?" Her eyebrows furrowed.

"We currently have a truce, now show me what you can do."

"Since when?" She grumbled, then got to work. Setting the coordinates and calculating the fuel, she prepared the ship to fly. She sent the ship sailing through space towards a small moon. Focusing on the target, she spoke. "Why'd you give me that translator? I know it wasn't cheap."

"You reminded me of my first mission, completely unprepared." I didn't mention the part where there was an untraceable GPS installed in the translator. I wanted to see her again. Her beauty and bravery on that shuttle had piqued my interest. Not to mention, humans were rare in these parts, and the only other way to see one was on Grihan. There was no way I'd spend the insane amount of credits necessary to see a human again, not when the most extraordinary one was nearby.

"Well thank you, I didn't get to say it back then."

I returned her thanks with a gentle squeeze to her hand. I didn't want to ruin her image of me.

"Fly around those asteroids," I said, pointing to a cluster stuck in the blue moon's orbit. She navigated through, turning the ship in time to avoid an asteroid with expert precision. Swinging the ship back around, she set the autopilot back on.

"Told ya." Her face beamed.

I sat back rubbing my hand along my jaw. *This might just work.* If I could get her to pilot while I sneaked into the Renari ship, I would have a much better chance of accomplishing my mission.

"You need money to get home, right? If you help me with a teeny task, I'll pay you handsomely." I turned her chair to face mine.

"Let me guess, it's for something illegal?"

"Fifty-thousand."

"I'm not going to help you break the la-"

"One-hundred-thousand."

"I don't even know yo-"

"Two-hundred-thousand, final offer."

She sat silent, her eyes calculating. Getting back to her planet would not be a cheap endeavor. If she kept working as a bounty hunter, it could end up taking her years just to scrounge up enough. I had just offered her the deal of a lifetime. I just hoped she was smart enough to take it. We sat in silence for a bit longer, until her eyes finally met mine.

"Three-hundred-thousand. But how do I know you'll stay true to your word? You didn't gain that bounty by being honest," she said as her eyebrows pinched together.

"Deal. I'll be the one out *working*, while you stay here on my ship. If anyone's at a disadvantage on this deal, it's me."

"And you trust me why?"

"Because I know the look of someone willing to do whatever it takes." Standing from the seat, I took a couple steps towards the door, then turned. "Now let's figure out where you'll be staying in the meantime."

STEALTH CAME at the cost of size. While my ship was large enough for one, two was a crowd. After hours of planning, we decided to call it a night. I gave Val my bed, taking the floor in the weapons room instead. *It's because I don't want her throwing my knives at me.* I shifted uncomfortably on the hard floor, the only padding being a sheer blanket. Who was I fooling? The prickly human was growing on me. Honestly, I was impressed with how far she'd made it in this universe. It wasn't an easy feat. If this mission went well, I would be spending the rest of my days on the beaches of Eirat.

I wonder if Val likes the beach.

I stopped myself there. After this mission, we would go our separate ways. It was the best for both of us. I tossed again, staring at the ceiling, unable to sleep on the cold floor.

Val threw off my morning routine entirely. After tossing and turning all night, I made my way to the bathroom only for it to be occupied.

Steam escaping through the door, I knocked once.

"Just a minute!" Val said, opening the door, the heat escaping into the hall.

"Are you trying to boil yourself?" I waved my hand, dispersing the steam.

"I wouldn't expect an alien with such delicate skin to understand." She stepped out, wearing only my shirt, our scents mingling. *I could get used to this.* It was huge on her; the hem reached her knees, leaving only her shapely calves exposed.

"Darling, if anyone is an alien, it's you. You're lightyears away from home." I shooed her out of the bathroom, craving the heat on my sore muscles. I set the temperature lower and hopped in the shower. Only one more rotation till the heist. I just hoped that Val would be able to make good on her promise.

After my shower, I headed towards the bridge, stopping when the sound of tinkling metal caught my attention. Opening the door to the weapons room, I watched as Val removed a knife from the wall. She tested the weight of it, and with a flick of her wrist she threw it at a crate. With a *clank*, the knife lodged itself into the metal of the crate. She turned, eyes wide and a smile on her face. "What is this made out of? I've never seen a knife cut through metal."

I pulled the knife out of the crate, inspecting

it for any chips. "It's Alderian obsidian, and it's *mine.*" Assuring that it was undamaged, I returned it to its place on the wall.

"I knew Alderians were possessive, but you take it to a whole other level." She reached for another knife.

I grabbed her wrist, stopping her, my face inches away. Her eyes widened, searching mine for my next move.

"I've already been generous enough with my food and my clothes. If you want Alderian obsidian, pay for it yourself." I let go of her wrist and her face sank a little. She forced her expression back into a neutral one and spun towards the door, her hands held behind her.

"Well then, we better get to making money," she said, walking into the hallway.

The rest of the day was spent on the bridge, working over the schematics of the Renari ship for what felt like the hundredth time.

"I'm telling you, we cut the engines and coast towards the ship, making it impossible for their cannons to pick up on us," Val said, pointing towards the cannons on the hologram of the ship.

"Yes, but it would make it difficult for you to get to the other ship in time to pick me up. You should fly in, I'll jump off in a suit, then you circle around to pick me back up."

"There's no way I can avoid that much

cannon fire. We'll be lucky to make it out alive," she said, her forehead wrinkling.

I flicked her forehead where the wrinkles met.

"Ouch! What was that for?" She covered her forehead with her hand.

"Sorry, I didn't mean to hit you that hard, let me check." I held her face in my hands. The contrast between my large hands and her small face made her feel even more delicate. I was starting to understand why Alderian males would spend exorbitant amounts for moments like this.

"Hmm looks fine to me," I said, turning her face left to right. I then swiftly brought my forehead to hers, headbutting her.

"What the hell?!" Her hands flew back up to her forehead.

"Stop doubting yourself, if you could make it on that shuttle back then, you can do this too." I tapped my finger against my head, smiling. "Also need to work on toughening up your head."

Still with her hand to her head, she looked up at me glowering. "You know on Earth a hard head means you're stupidly stubborn."

My chest rumbled with laughter. "Then it looks like you have no choice but to go with my plan, don't you?"

Val's only response was a soft clicking of her tongue and a deep sigh. She focused back on the schematics for the next several hours, memorizing everything down to the smallest detail. Once we were both satisfied with the amount of information we had obtained, we made our way to bed, hoping we were prepared for the next day.

SEVENTEEN

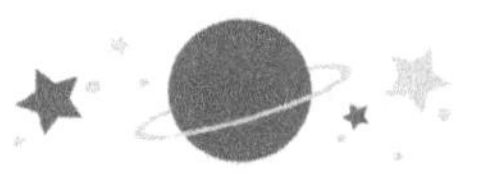

Star System 73

VAL

"Ready?" Te'ryn asked through the small speaker in the cockpit of his ship.

I took in a breath, checking the controls on the ship again, totally sure everything was set correctly. *So far so good.* I checked the black landscape in front of me. A distant silver carrier stuck out like a sore thumb against the darkness of space around it. The Renari ship was on time. Preparing myself for action, I looked at the screen to the side of me. The visuals through Te'ryn's feed were clear. He was crouched on top of the ship suited up—waiting for my signal.

"Ready."

I hit the thrusters of the ship. The engines roared to life, sending us flying towards the Renari carrier. "Woop Woop!" I heard Te'ryn's cheer through the line.

"You're fucking crazy," I groaned, as my grip tightened. Forty seconds till they noticed us.

"You're on this ship with me darling. Whether you admit it or not, you're not entirely sane either."

If I ever make it back to Earth I'll need an insane amount of therapy.

Ten seconds. I readied myself.

Five.

Te'ryn leaped from the ship. He spiraled behind, disappearing from view. Just when I thought he was gone, he ignited the jets in his suit shooting him towards the carrier.

Now!

Blasts of bright yellow shot out from the carrier. I spun the ship avoiding two of the blasts. Three more blasts shot my way. I pushed the ship down, my hair falling forward over my shoulders. The two blasts nearly hit the wing. Too close for comfort. *Come on, you got this.* The ship alarms blared and I whipped my head to the right. The third blast spiraled towards me.

Blinded by the yellow light heading towards me, I hit the thrusters harder veering to the left.

Woosh.

The final blast flew past. I kept the thrusters at full power as I circled back creating distance between me and the Renari carrier. Now safely out of range, I turned my attention to Te'ryn's feed.

The view on the screen was black. I waited, watching with bated breath.

"What's your status?" I asked after a couple minutes.

"Are you checking to see if I'm still alive?" Te'ryn whispered.

"Well, are you? I can't see anything."

"That's because I'm currently hiding in a supply closet." Te'ryn kept his voice low.

"Are you sure you're a professional? Maybe I should cut my losses now," I said, emphasizing the last sentence.

"If you take my ship, I swear I'll find you. And you won't like me when I do."

Te'ryn opened the door, showing an illuminated hallway. Two armed Renari guards paced down the hallway. Their luminescent gold scaled skin peeked out from their black uniforms. Te'ryn's daggers sailed through the air landing perfectly in the crack between their uniforms and helmets.

I was reminded of how easily he'd taken out the bodyguards on the shuttle. *This guy is bad news, maybe I should bail while I can.* I breathed shakily as I watched him free his daggers from the guards' necks with ease. *Maybe it's best not to piss this guy off.*

"I hardly doubt you could find me in a sea of humans." I forced a laugh.

"Darling, I could find a blade of grass in a

field," Te'ryn said as he continued down the hallway.

"Uh huh, sure." My focus snapped back to the ship in front of me. Sentries scanned the surrounding area looking for me.

"Better pick up the pace." I turned my attention back to Te'ryn.

"Patience is necessary to obtain optimal results," he said, the irritation clear in his voice.

"Oh watch out, you almost sounded human there," I said, watching him turn down another hallway. As he stepped into view, two guards aimed their comically large blasters at him. Before they could pull the trigger, Te'ryn had already taken them down. I swallowed the lump in my throat as I watched. *Once you get the money you can leave and forget this ever happened.*

"Well I wouldn't want that, would I? It would make me sound too *alien.*" He chuckled at his own joke as he pushed a dead guard's hand against the door's scanner. After a *beep*, the door slid open revealing a brightly lit white room on the other side. In the center, sat a floating large blue stone. "Val, get ready for part two." He reached for the gem.

I hit the thrusters again propelling the ship forward and zooming past a small sentry. Not missing a beat, it spun locking on to my ship.

"Shit." I swore under my breath as four other sentries followed in pursuit.

"Breathe, you got this," Te'ryn said as he ran down a corridor, colliding with several more armed guards.

"I told you this was a bad idea!" My voice cracked as I narrowly avoided another blast.

Gunshots sounded from Te'ryn's feed. I moved my gaze from the view outside to the screen. A guard grappled with Te'ryn, pulling him to the ground. He quickly grabbed the guard by his collar, flinging him over his head.

"Te'ryn, you have four minutes till I'm in position," I said, dodging another blast.

"I'm working on it," Te'ryn grunted, throwing another guard off him, then stabbing him in the neck. Several more guards flooded the hallway, surrounding him completely.

"Three minutes," I gasped as a guard rammed Te'ryn in the head with the butt of his gun. Te'ryn let out a groan and spun, ripping the gun out of the guard's hands.

"Two minutes, come on Te'ryn." I watched as another guard tackled him, the feed showing only the ground beneath him. He looked up and the screen filled with the sight of a guard holding a blaster point blank at Te'ryn's head.

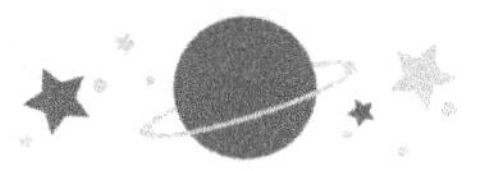

Star System 73

TE'RYN

I struggled against the weight of the Renari guard on top of me.

"Don't move," the other guard barked, his blaster pointed directly at me.

I steeled myself, counting the guards around me.

Twelve.

I had moved too slow, giving them a chance to corner me. I inhaled, calming my pulse. I had to play my cards right. I would act subdued then make a break for it when their guard was down. I looked back at the guard with the blaster. His face was covered by an ornate helmet, making it impossible to make out his expression.

Must be the captain. Either he was planning on killing me now, or locking me up to find out what I knew. *My credits are on the latter.* To my surprise the captain knelt down and removed my helmet, pulling the earpiece out of my ear. His helmet retracted, showing his golden scaled face, black curved horns and signature Renari red slitted eyes.

He put the earpiece in his own ear and spoke. "Surrender or the Alderian dies."

My eyes widened. No way they would get Val to agree to that. She had already escaped one captor, there was no way she would risk her freedom. "Good luck with that," I let out a snort.

The Renari's head tilted to the side. "I guess I should have known better than to expect loyalty among petty criminals." His talon flexed on the trigger.

I closed my eyes.

Still alive a few seconds later, I cracked an eye open. The guard stood with his talon on the trigger, but now held another to his ear. A tight smile spread across his thin lips, the scales around his cheeks glinting in the light.

"Looks like there is some loyalty after all. Lock him up," he ordered the others, marching away as a guard pulled me to my feet.

Why? The question rang in my head as the guards threw me into a glass cell. I stumbled in, bracing myself on my hands and knees, catching myself before colliding with the floor. Val had every reason to leave. Why had she given herself up for a complete stranger? A stranger she had once tried to capture for a bounty? I thought I had a grasp of how humans worked, but now, I felt like everything I knew was wrong. The sound of marching feet filled the corridor, and I turned my attention to the incoming guards.

There in between two guards, was Val with her hands held behind her back, eyes downcast and brown hair disheveled. The guards approached my cell. The glass slid apart, and a guard tossed Val into the cell, closing it behind him. Before I could catch her, Val's shoulder hit the ground with a soft *thud.*

"We meet again, floor." She rolled to her back, avoiding my gaze.

"It seems you and the floor have a history," I said softly, not sure what to say.

"Yeah, a long history of heartbreak," she said with a scoff.

"Thank you," I said, my eyes finally meeting hers. Dark circles sat beneath her eyes, their green color duller than usual. She struggled to sit up; I grabbed her hand and pulled her next to me.

"Yeah, well, I couldn't add more names to my list." She looked away. I leaned in closer to her.

"List of what?"

"People I disappointed," she said, turning

back towards me, her face only a hair's width away from mine.

She was incredible. In all my time, I had never met someone as good-hearted nor as beautiful as her. My world felt too vile for her, but my desire to know what her lips felt like against mine won out against what little conscience I had.

I leaned in farther, desperate to find out what her lips tasted like. Would they taste as sweet as she smelled?

Before I could find out, she pulled back. I felt her weight push against my side as she let her muscles relax an inch.

"I don't think I qualify for that list since I'm an *alien* and all." I smiled, trying to coax my snarky human back. She let a tiny puff of air escape her nose.

"You should feel honored, not many aliens make it off my kick-their-ass list."

"What list am I on now, if not either of those?" I asked, nudging her shoulder.

"I'm still trying to figure that out."

I let a laugh ring out at her reply. Splaying my legs out in front of me, I pulled her down with a gentle tug, resting her head on my thighs. She tensed, her head hovering a few inches above my thigh. I traced my fingers along the green and blue bruises now appearing along her shoulder. *I'll kill a Renari for each bruise.* She'd given herself up to save my life, it was the least I could do.

"What now?" She let her head drop, resting it on my lap.

"You tell me, you're the escape artist."

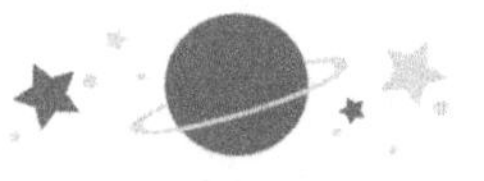

NINETEEN

Star System 72

VAL

The long nights of planning had finally caught up with me. I no longer had the energy to come up with a plan nor figure out why I was using Te'ryn's legs as a pillow. Not only did I barely know the man—alien, whatever, but I had no idea who, or what he was. I was reminded of how quickly he downed the bodyguards on the shuttle and the Renari ship. He had the speed and grace of someone who had done it enough to perfect the movements. He had more red flags than a communist parade. I should be running, not cuddling.

Also, his thighs are rock hard.

My thoughts eventually quieted and even with the uncomfortable pillow, I fell into a deep slumber.

Steps echoed down the hallway, and I woke up with a start. Mumbling and wiping the sleep from my eyes, I focused my sight to see where the oncoming noise was coming from. Te'ryn placed his hand on my shoulder and I jolted, still not fully alert.

"It's just me, Val."

"I know, I'm just, ugh..." Feeling as though I had been hit by a truck, I rolled my achy shoulder, failing to stretch the sore muscles. I was too old to be sleeping on hard floors. I watched as three armed guards passed by, their heads turning to stare at me.

"I take it they've never seen a human before," I said under my breath.

"Not many *aliens* have, your kind is pretty rare around these parts." Te'ryn stood, wiping invisible dust off his trousers.

"But you knew what I was, why?" I turned my gaze from the guards to him.

"I had business on Grihan, and became acquainted with a female of your species." Te'ryn picked invisible hair off his shirt.

One eyebrow raised, I rested a hand on my hip. "Acquainted?" I don't know why it mattered to me, but I was now curious.

"Oh, are you jealous?"

"No, but it must have been an important talk for you to part with your precious credits."

"It wasn't, but I had to meet with, uh, a client there," Te'ryn said, turning his attention to incoming guards.

The golden Renari captain that had captured Te'ryn approached, holding a small metal case. The captain stopped, holding his hand with long black claws up, signaling the other guards to come to a standstill. Te'ryn folded his arms, his large biceps flexing as he towered over the Renari. I took a step behind him, careful to keep the captain in sight.

"I thought we just captured a petty thief, but it seems like you've been branching out of your normal *activities*," the captain said, opening the case.

Inside was an Alderian obsidian dagger. The familiar jagged curves and silver handles matched the other daggers Te'ryn frequently used. The captain picked it up, inspecting it in the light. "This was found in the heart of our crown prince."

A guard handed him an almost identical dagger. "And this was found on your person, care to explain?" The captain's ruby red eyes flickered almost as if a fire burned inside.

Te'ryn shrugged nonchalantly. "Must be a common design."

"You can lie as much as you want, but we *will* find out the truth." The captain pounded his fist against the glass. I jumped and his attention moved to me. His gaze lingered on me for a moment then returned to Te'ryn.

"Due to our treaty with the Federation you'll have to be handed over to them first before we can investigate you." He looked upset at the political red tape stopping him from skewering Te'ryn with his dangerously sharp looking claws. "As for the-"

He paused, looking over me as if he could find an answer written across my forehead. "As for the *developing species*, no empire, nor Federation has you under their protection. Therefore, you'll be taken to Rena to be prosecuted as our law sees fit."

I grabbed the back of Te'ryn's shirt, my knuckles white. He reached a hand behind him, giving me a comforting squeeze. With a burst of confidence, I met the captain's eyes. "Surely flying around your ship in a free star system isn't criminal?"

He smiled as if a child had tried to convince him the sky was green. "No, but assisting a criminal that assassinated our crown prince and who also attempted to steal our crown jewel, is. You two may remain together until we reach Rena." He disappeared through the doors—ending the conversation.

My head whipped up, locking eyes with

Te'ryn. Conscious of being overheard, I looked out towards the doors, then at Te'ryn, raising an eyebrow. *Did you kill the crown prince?* I asked him wordlessly. He returned my gaze, pressing his eyes up into crescents with a slight shrug.

Oh my god he totally did.

I let out a groan, grabbing my head. I should have known, all the signs pointed to this. I cursed my self for being so stupid.

"God, I have such terrible taste in men." I sat in the corner, back facing Te'ryn.

I heard his footsteps approach. "I'm an alien, remember?" He flashed me a smile but his face drooped when I didn't react. He sat next to me, careful not to touch. "I can go back to being a quack doctor if you want."

I let out a snort. "It's a little too late for that."

"But I am your taste, even if your preferences are bad?" His eyes twinkled as he smiled.

"I'm a new woman now, my tastes have officially changed." I held his gaze, refusing to look away first.

"For you, Val, I would prescribe as many fake medicines as possible, since that is apparently what you desire in a male," Te'ryn said, holding one hand extended, another over his heart.

"Stop. That is not-" I hit his chest, holding down a smile. *Don't laugh at his jokes, remember you're mad at him.*

He pulled me towards him. "I would even open up my own clinic, devoted to studying the anatomy of the *elusive* humans."

He was so close I could feel his breath on my cheek.

"But in this scenario you're still a quack, so you would confuse an Azzek for a human." I tilted my head, smiling.

"I would never." His voice rose an octave as his face moved closer.

"I will get you out of here, Val, I promise," he said, back to his low voice.

Stay strong Val, he may be handsome but he is dangero—my thought got cut off as he pressed his lips against mine. Ignoring the blaring sirens in my head, I leaned into him, parting my mouth. His hand pushed against the back of my head pulling me closer. Te'ryn's tongue slid between my lips, tangling with my own.

As if he just found water after days without, Te'ryn's kisses intensified, turning to gentle bites across my bottom lip as he slowly pulled away.

"Val, trust me." He breathed heavily. Before I could reply, his mouth crashed into mine again, filling the empty space he previously created.

My hands wrapped around his large frame drawing him closer. Our kisses became deeper and he grabbed my ass, bringing me on top of his lap into a straddle. I could feel his excitement beneath me. I moaned as his kisses moved across my neck.

"Tell me you want me as much as I want you," he said, as his hand moved up my rib cage. He waited for me to answer.

I did want him, I really did. He was like a magnet and I couldn't resist him, no matter how dangerous he was. I nodded, giving him the okay.

His hand moved up exploring my body, stopping as he brushed against the dagger I had "borrowed" and strapped around my ribs.

"Oh, you've been a bad girl." His fingers circled the dagger, causing goosebumps to appear across my skin.

"Good thing I like that."

His hands slid lower, resting gently on my waist. Out of the corner of my eye, I spotted several guards standing around, their attention focused solely on us.

"Maybe we should wait." I stared into his now ravenous eyes.

His attention turned to an even larger group of guards now gathered, watching the spectacle. My cheeks burned red. Te'ryn cleared his throat, lifting me off him.

"Let's continue this when our nosey neighbors are gone," he whispered into my ear.

I gave him a nod, too embarrassed to meet his or the guards' eyes. *I don't need therapy, I need the psych ward.*

TWENTY

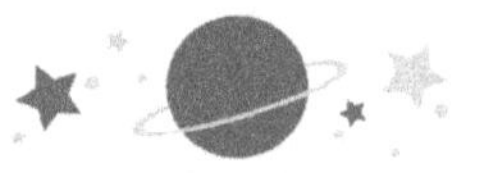

Star System 57

TE'RYN

V al was full of surprises. One being that she tasted amazing. The other was that she was a lot sneakier than I thought. Luckily her tiny grabby hands would make it possible to get us out of here. I felt her rhythmic breaths against me as I held her sleeping body close.

I wonder if she would like the dunes of Heldath. I was sure her large eyes would sparkle at the sight of the glittering multi-colored sands that filled the planet. Once we got out of here, maybe we could make a detour. My heart sank. Of course she couldn't, she would stick out like a sore thumb. She didn't belong on this side of the universe. And I belonged alone, that's what worked best. I forced my thoughts back to the escape plan.

Val stirred awake. I whispered into her ear. "Are you ready to kick ass today?"

I slid my hand up to the dagger strapped around her. She stiffened up. *One step back.* I brought my hand back down.

"Uh yeah, I'm always ready to kick ass," she said groggily.

"Then can I have my dagger back?"

"Mmm I suppose so." She slid the dagger into my hand.

"How generous of you." I took the dagger. Eyeing the passing guards, I made sure to keep my movements small, transferring it to my pocket.

"Follow my lead." I gave Val a wink.

Her eyebrows pinched in return as she watched me. I stood up, pacing the room, waiting for the food rations to be delivered. Minutes later, a tray with two *Dhale* bars slid through the small opening in the glass.

"Oh great, sand," Val said, making a face.

I held one out to her. "What, they're nutritious and filling, there's worse things you could be eating."

She grabbed the *Dhale* bar and took tiny bites out of it, giving up halfway. "What could be worse than this?"

"Trash." I took the half-eaten bar and finished it.

Val gave me a look and opened her mouth, but decided against saying anything. It was better that way. I had already made her nervous with my *profession*, better to not add a sob story on top of it.

Since when do I care what someone thinks? I'd never once tried to hide what—who I was, until Val. *It's because I need her cooperation, that's why.* At least, that's what I told myself.

"Actually it tastes about the same." I stuck my tongue out at Val, receiving a laugh in return. Taking the empty tray, I placed it by the opening.

A passing guard noticed the empty tray and reached into the cell. Before the guard could react, I swung the dagger down, pinning his hand to the floor. Val let out a yelp, and the guard groaned in pain. Moving quickly, I pulled the guard's hand farther through the hole. "Open the door if you want to keep your arm."

He scrambled for his blaster, but with another tug, his face collided with the glass. He gave up on fighting me and slapped his hand against the scanner, opening the door. I stepped through the entrance as the guard tried in vain to free his hand. He pulled his blaster out and swung it in my direction, but he was too slow. I flung the dagger into his neck, sending him to the floor. Pulling my dagger free, I turned to Val. Her hands trembled as she stared at me with wide eyes.

"Don't you want to go home, Val?" I tilted my head.

She closed her eyes for a moment then took a breath, steadying herself. "Okay, let's do this." She followed after me. "Just try to keep the killing to a minimum please."

"Don't worry, I try not to work when I'm not getting paid." I handed Val the deceased guard's gun, and set off down the hallway towards the *Heart of the Renari.*

"You don't consider this part of the job?" She readied her blaster.

"No, this is overtime." I took out another guard, catching him before he turned the corner. Val gave the dead guard a wide berth and followed me closely down the hall. Following the path I memorized, we made our way back to the room holding the *Heart.*

Two guards stood before the door. I motioned to Val to keep quiet while I ran towards them. Dodging the shots fired, I took out the guard on the right. The second guard took aim, but I swung my leg out, kicking his feet out from beneath him. He fell to the ground with a *thud* and I delivered the finishing blow. Using the guard, I opened the door to the room with the *Heart.* As I reached for it, I heard the steps of more approaching soldiers. Quickly sliding the *Heart of the Renari* into my jacket, I turned to greet the newcomers. Two more guards raced towards us from the end of the corridor. Val stood ready with her back to me, blaster in position.

Before one guard could pull the trigger, my dagger had already found its way into his neck. The other guard turned to fire but Val shot him just below the belt, sending him to the ground with a howl.

"Now that's just cruel," I remarked, grabbing the blaster out of Val's shaking hands.

I stood over the guard, pointing the blaster at his head. His wide eyes stared at me with fear, and I pulled the trigger. "Good thing I gave you another opportunity to make credits, because bounty hunting is not for you, Val."

I handed the blaster back to Val, her unsteady hands nearly dropping it.

"Bounty hunting doesn't involve so much killing," she said through gritted teeth.

"In an ideal galaxy, maybe." I pushed her forward and started to run. I turned the corner and she followed as we sprinted through the hallways. The sound of more footsteps echoed down the hall. Grabbing her by the waist, I pulled Val into a small supply closet. Chest to chest, I could feel Val's quick heartbeats against me. Hearing the guards approach, I put a hand over Val's mouth. The footsteps passed, and I removed it. Val took a deep breath, as her hands restlessly fiddled with her blaster.

"We're almost to the dock, I can do this," she whispered.

I leaned in. "You're doing amazing." I ran my thumb along her cheek. I felt pride swell for my tiny human. She clearly had no experience with so much death, but she was still trying to be brave.

After checking that the coast was clear, we made our way out of the closet. We followed the twisting corridors, dashing till we made it to the dock. We took our time approaching, cautiously taking each step as guards shuffled through the halls. I motioned for Val to take cover behind some crates. I watched behind our cover as more guards filled the room, each armed with a large blaster. They'd been notified of our escape attempt. They scanned the room, looking for any sign of movement.

Keeping my voice low, I drew Val close. "I'll distract them, you get to the ship and I'll meet you there."

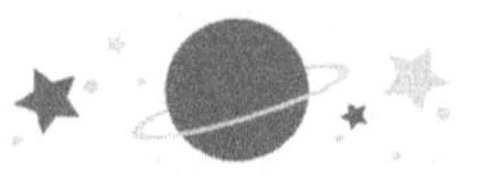

TWENTY-ONE

Star System 55

VAL

I watched through the crack between crates as Te'ryn took off towards the nearest group of guards. Yelling and gunshots filled the room. Making sure all was clear, I sprinted towards Te'ryn's ship. Guards surrounded Te'ryn as he fought using only his dagger and various guards as alien-shields.

As I neared the ship, I focused on moving forward. *Just a little farther.* I reassured myself as shouting and blaster noise grew louder around me. Almost to the ship, I suddenly felt a sharp pain in my arm. I turned my head to see a guard with his blaster pointed at me. He fired another shot, dropping me to my knees, narrowly missing being hit by the second shot. Blood dripped down my arm, causing the heavy blaster to slip from my hand. I gripped it tighter and steadied the blaster in my hand, aiming towards the Renari guard. Before I could pull the trigger, my finger locked. My panic stopped me from taking the shot.

Cursing my moment of weakness, I dodged as the guard fired another shot. He didn't let up and kept firing in my direction. I felt another sharp pain strike my thigh and my knee buckled. I fell and rolled across the ground, barely avoiding another hit. The guard rushed forward and I pulled myself up. Swinging the blaster in his direction, I pulled the trigger as soon as he was in range.

The guard fell. Black blood pooled out from a large wound in his chest.

I thought I was ready to do anything to get home, but now I wasn't so sure. I watched as the guard's labored breaths finally ceased. It felt as if all the air in the room had been sucked out. I struggled to take a breath as my chest tightened. He must have hit me there because it felt like I was dying. My hand slowly moved up as I struggled to breathe, finding no blood. *I must be in shock, I'm dying.* My thoughts turned towards home—Earth. I was never going to get back. I felt a hand on my shoulder, snapping me back into the present.

"It was him or you, Val. You did what you had to do." Te'ryn sounded as if he was miles away. "*Vaat*, you're injured. Hold your hand here, okay? I'm going to carry you."

Te'ryn pushed my hand against the wound in my arm, lifting me up into his arms.

I felt Te'ryn's chest rise and fall as he carried me into his ship. He sat me down in the co-pilot's chair, strapping the seatbelts over me. "Hold on Val, I'm going to get us out of here and then we can patch you up."

The ship's engines roared to life beneath us, and I felt the force of take off.

"Hang in there Val," Te'ryn said as he took a sharp turn, avoiding fire from the ships following close behind. An impact shook the ship. "*Vaat!*" Te'ryn swore as alarms sounded.

The ship spun out of control, sending us plummeting towards a small gray planet.

"VAL, WAKE UP!" I felt the pull of Te'ryn's hands, releasing me from my seat.

My body struggled to move, and every muscle screamed in pain. I held onto Te'ryn's shirt as he steadied me, helping me through the dark ship. My foot caught on something and I fell forward. Te'ryn caught me before I hit the floor, pulling me under his arm.

"You can't even see in the dark? How does your species survive?" He held me close, guiding me to the crack of light seeping through the door.

"No, that's why we invented emergency lights, unlike your people," I shot back, helping Te'ryn push open the door.

"Seems like you're in okay shape since you're able to talk back."

I rolled my eyes. Before I could retort, a blast of cold air hit us as the door swung open. A shiver ran through my body as I took in the scenery around us. Gray rocks splattered the gray dirt, contrasting with the black of the sky behind it. The only thing in sight other than the barren landscape was a small bunker embedded into the land, and what looked to be some sort of rusty digging machine.

My head felt light and my legs swayed beneath me. *I must have lost more blood than I thought.* Noticing my lack of stability, Te'ryn slammed the door shut.

"Sit down before you faint." I felt the push on my shoulders helping me to the ground.

Te'ryn took off down the hall as I focused on my breathing. He returned shortly, putting a helmet over my head. Oxygen filled my lungs, and I felt steady again.

"You humans really are weak." He shook his head.

"Since I saved your ass, what does that make you?" I weakly slapped his shoulder.

He chuckled and picked me up from the floor. Still in his arms, Te'ryn pushed the door open, jumping down to the gray earth.

"I can walk now." I wiggled as his grip tightened.

"No way, I have to prove to you that I'm not weak," he said with a wink. We made our way to the bunker, shivering the whole way.

As we arrived at the bunker, my shivering increased. Te'ryn tried to open the door but it didn't budge. He tried again, pulling harder, forcing the door open an inch. After setting me down and pushing with all his might, Te'ryn managed to get the door open enough for the both of us.

"Shall we?" He held his hand out. I took it.

"Only because I can't see in the dark," I said under my breath.

"Hold on, I can fix that." Te'ryn fumbled with a wall panel. "*Vaating* old mining equipment." He smacked the panel, causing the room to fill with light. Sand coated the gray room's floor. The room was mostly empty save for some chairs and a tilted table.

"Tell me why we have to stay in this creepy place instead of the ship?"

"Because the engine has been compromised, and I'd rather be outside than inside if it decides to explode," Te'ryn said, pulling his tattered jacket over my shaking shoulders. "Stay here, I'll get us supplies and something to keep us warm." He disappeared down another hallway.

I rubbed my hands together trying to bring back some of the warmth. I was now stuck on an abandoned mining planet with a dangerous assassin. *An assassin I kissed.* I covered my face with my hands. My position had gone from bad to worse. Luckily it seemed like Te'ryn had no intentions of killing me, *yet.* He seemed far more interested in flirting. And he was a great kisser. A puff of air escaped my nose. I thought I had my fair share of crazy life events, but the universe loved to prove me wrong.

Te'ryn returned. "I found an old bedroom we can set up while we figure out how to get off."

"How are we going to do that exactly?" I followed him down the shadowy corridor.

The small circular room held a small cot and another old rusty chair. I kicked the cot, sending dust flying into the air.

"What was that for?" Te'ryn coughed.

"Making sure there aren't any weird alien parasites." I eyed the cot, watching for movement.

Te'ryn sat down on the cot leaning his back against the wall. "The only alien on this planet is me, Val, this place has been abandoned for years."

"And yet you're the most dangerous one I've met," I mumbled, sitting beside him.

"But, I'm the most handsome right?" He smiled. I turned my head, focusing on the chair. I would *not* fall for that smile again. Te'ryn placed his hands on the helmet and pulled it off my head. "The filters are on, it's safe to take this off."

I took a cautious breath. Other than the dust in the air, I could breathe just fine. I felt his hands pull down the jacket, exposing my shoulders. I turned, meeting his eyes.

"Just trying to take a look at that wound you've got, nothing else." He removed his hands, waiting for permission to continue. I slipped the jacket off, offering him my injured arm.

"Why are you being so nice?"

He held my arm gently inspecting the wound. "It isn't too deep, it should be okay in the meantime." He pulled the jacket back up "You came back to save me, even though I'm practically a stranger." His silver eyes looked up at me gleaming in the dim light. "I don't take that lightly, Val." He leaned in closer, his face only inches from mine.

"Yeah, well you're too pretty. You wouldn't last a day in prison." I gave him a smirk, my gaze catching on his lips. Would it be so bad to kiss him again? We could just have a no-strings-attached thing, and when I got my cut of the credits, I could leave everything behind. "Consider it charity." I met his eyes.

We held each other's gazes for a while, hesitant to pull away. My breath hitched as he began to shift. "Well thank you for the *charity*, jumpsuits look awful on me by the way, so you really did me a favor." He leaned in closer, catching my lips with his.

Hungry for more, I pressed against him, my kisses becoming more intense. Te'ryn grasped around my waist pulling me on top of him. His hands explored my body, slipping underneath my makeshift shirt-dress.

"What are you doing to me, Val?" He mumbled as he kissed down my neck.

I didn't know what it was either, but I couldn't resist Te'ryn's pull. He teased me as he continued to kiss along my collarbone, brushing his hands along my sides. Desperate for more, I leaned into him, giving him permission. I was hungry for his touch.

His hands slid higher.

"Te'ryn." I gasped as he grabbed my breast, massaging it.

His other hand pushed against my hips, causing me to grind against the bulge in his pants. Heat pooled in my stomach, and I rocked harder against him. He grabbed the bottom of my shirt-dress, pulling it up. The shirt caught on my bad arm, causing me to let out a small yelp. Te'ryn froze at the noise.

"You should rest, Val."

He pulled back and helped me off him as he laid down on the cot. He patted the space next to him.

Disappointment hit, and I was surprised at my reaction. D*on't get involved, you're leaving,* I reminded myself as I laid next to him. The small cot creaked beneath our weight. I wasn't sure if it could hold the large Alderian who was now taking up the majority of the space. My worries about the stability of the cot melted away along with the cold in my limbs as I snuggled closer to Te'ryn.

Survival 101: huddle for warmth, that's all this is. He pulled a blanket over us, trapping in his warmth. The heat was all I needed because I quickly fell asleep.

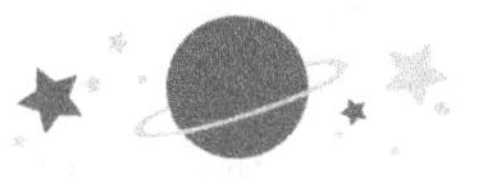

TWENTY-TWO

Star System 54

TE'RYN

I woke up with Val in my arms. I nuzzled my face into her hair, filling my nostrils with her sweet scent. *All the credits on Alderi could never purchase this feeling.* Maybe I could disguise Val as an Undrian again and take her to see the Celestial Rings of Talma. She would love the sweet food that filled the stalls in the city there. *Surely she can spare a couple extra days before making the journey back to her planet?* Happy with my plan I decided to bring it up as soon as she woke up. Val seemed to need more sleep than I, so I left the cot slowly, making sure not to wake her.

I made my way back to my ship, the smoke now dissipated from the torn wing. With a low groan, the door slid open. "Seventy-thousand credits down the drain." I sighed, giving the door frame a pat.

I entered the weapons room taking in the

mess around me. All my weapons had fallen off their places on the wall. Crates laid open and the contents I had collected throughout the years were scattered across the floor. I started to pick up the mess and re-equipped my daggers. A sense of comfort returned, I felt naked without them. After I finished with the quick clean-up, I dumped out a chest filled with tools for the ship. I pulled more daggers and blasters off the wall and started to fill the chest with items I would need. Val's container of blue paint and old earpiece caught my attention. I held the earpiece up, inspecting it. A small blue light illuminated one side—it was still active. I could call her bounty-hunting buddies, surely they could come get her. I ruminated on the idea.

That would be best, but then we'd have to part ways sooner than I would have liked. They probably wouldn't let her out on any missions after this, even though she could clearly hold her own.

My grip tightened.

But then she would be safe. I relaxed my hand, tossing the paint into the crate and slid the earpiece into my pocket.

I returned to the bunker, crate in hand. I found Val digging through some old lockers. "Find anything good?" I set the crate down, sending a cloud of dust up into the air.

"Nope, just more dust." She coughed.

"Perfect, I was worried we were going to run out." I opened the crate, pulling out several weapons, and began inspecting them for damage.

"Har har." Val reached for the crate. I stopped her, grabbing her hand.

"Uh, uh, didn't your mom teach you not to touch others belongings?"

"Didn't your mom teach you to share?" She pulled her hand back, but I refused to let go.

"No, she taught me to protect what's mine," I growled. I pulled her into me, lips crashing against hers.

"Te'ryn, wait, we have to work on getting out of here," she breathed, backing away.

I ran my thumb along her lower lip. "We have time. Do you not want to?"

"That's not what I-"

I met her lips again, cutting off her words. I picked her up still kissing, her legs wrapping around me as I led us to the small cot. I adjusted my now erect cock as I laid Val beneath me. I took in the sight of her red cheeks, her plump lips and her starry eyes. I felt like the richest Alderian in the universe.

"*Vaat*, you are so beautiful." I slid my hand down from her cheek, feeling the smooth skin across her collar bones. She let out a small gasp as my hand slid farther down. "Only today, just give me one day," I breathed into her neck.

She gave a small nod and my self control evaporated.

I ripped the shirt—*my shirt* off her exposing her smooth curves. Goosebumps rose across her skin from the cold air. I kissed down reaching her pebbled nipple. I took it in my mouth, sucking and teasing. She let out a gasp and I felt a smile stretch across my face. "You're so easy to please."

Her hand gripped my hair, pulling my head up. "Please, you're going to have-" I slid my finger through her soft folds, then pushed up inside her. She moaned. The sound was music to my ears.

"Going to have to, what?" I slid another finger inside.

"To, ah…"

Pulling my fingers out, I licked the sweet liquid off. She tasted just as delicious as she smelled. I didn't let her finish talking before I pushed her legs up, diving into her soft mound, licking up more of her sweetness.

"Te'ryn, please," she moaned as I circled my tongue around her clit. I pressed my tongue harder against her. She let out another moan at my touch and I took my time enjoying her sweetness. She grabbed my hair, directing me to where she needed me. I would go wherever she wanted me, I was hers.

"I'm going to-" she said, as I felt her legs clench around me as she reached climax.

I propped myself up on my elbows, feeling a trickle of precum drip down my shaft. I stared down at the small human beneath me, her chest rose and fell with each deep breath.

My small human.

I was a fool for thinking this would be a one time thing. I needed her, every day, more than anything. I waited for the okay from Val. After receiving it, I pulled down my pants, freeing my cock. Val's eyes widened at the sight.

"What, too alien for you? Although your anatomy doesn't seem much different from females of my species." I circled her clit with my finger again, receiving another gasp.

"No, it's just big." Her small hand stroked my shaft, bringing it towards her.

I positioned my cock against her entrance, feeling her wetness against my tip. It was going to be difficult to keep from losing myself with how tight she was. But I didn't want to hurt her, so I would give her as much time as she needed.

"I'll be gentle, I promise. Now open your legs."

Her eyes met mine, full of need as she spread her legs for me. "I'll need a little more than that," she said, as I thrust inside. Moaning, her hands grasped my back, her nails digging into my skin.

"Naughty girl, I knew you'd want more." I thrust harder, her hips meeting mine. Val's moans of pleasure filled the air. I hit a steady rhythm and our kisses intensified, both of us desperate to be closer.

"Te'ryn!" Val screamed as my release filled her.

Not done enjoying each other's bodies yet, we spent the rest of the day in ecstasy. After just one taste of her, I was addicted. Like a silversalt junkie, I would never be able to let her go.

Val was *mine*, she just didn't know it yet.

TWENTY-THREE

Star System 54

VAL

"Okay, if you had to pick, would you rather have no arms or no legs?" I laid next to Te'ryn, his hands lazily stroking up and down my naked body. I took in his handsome face. We'd spent the previous hours wrapped up in each other. I was exhausted—in a good way.

"I thought we were trying to get to know each other better." I felt his laugh rumble against me.

"We are, this tells me what you consider important."

"Hmm, I'd probably go with missing one arm and one leg."

"Hold on, you only get two options, not three." I slapped his chest as he moved in closer, his hot breath brushing against my face.

"There's always a third choice," he said in a low voice. I stuck my tongue out at him. He pressed his lips against my mouth, then pulled back smiling. His eyebrows softened and he drew me in tighter. "What are you going to do when you get back to your planet?"

"Well, I'll have to look for a job, being missing for almost two years is a pretty good reason to get fired. And I'll have to find a new roommate, it was awkward before…and coming back with an abducted-by-aliens story will probably make it seem like I ran away." I focused on the gray ceiling, remembering how embarrassed I was to be around Steph after my confession.

She looked so concerned, probably worried she'd hurt my feelings. *"I only see you as a friend Val, I'm really sorry. But I don't want us to stop being friends. I promise I won't make it weird."* Steph's kindness almost made it worse. I would have preferred her being mean, that way I could have gotten over her easier. Funnily, it didn't hurt anymore. *I guess an alien abduction and a tryst with an assassin does that.*

"That's what you've been working so hard for? What's so important about a job?" Te'ryn placed his thumb under my chin, pushing my face up towards his.

"It's not my job that's important. I'd hardly call being a front end developer the most exciting thing. I just want to be able to go outside and feel the sun on my skin without being afraid someone might find out I'm a human. I want a normal life, one not full of fear, but freedom."

"So that's it? Just for a so-called normal life you'll go back to your disease-ridden planet and what, maybe live two hundred or so cycles?"

"Two-hundred? I'll only get a hundred—if I'm lucky." I laughed.

Te'ryn's eyes moved back and forth, thinking of what to say next. I forgot that with their technology, aliens lived much longer lives.

"Hey, it's not much, but it's my disease-ridden planet," I continued.

I didn't even know what to do with the rest of my life at thirty, I couldn't imagine having several hundred years tacked on to that.

"Val, have you thought about staying? Even for a human there's a lot here, I could help you find somewhere you're happy. At least that way you wouldn't have to die so young."

I sat up from the cot, looking for my— Te'ryn's shirt. "I don't belong here, all I am is a fancy toy to these aliens."

Te'ryn's arm wrapped around my waist, his head pushing into my back. "Not to this alien you're not," he mumbled.

"And that's why you're on my friend's-with-benefits list." I lifted his hands off me. Pulling the shirt over my head, I made my way out of the room, leaving Te'ryn on the cot behind me.

Stop it Val. Don't catch feelings.

I had to go home. I slapped my cheek, trying to stop my traitorous brain. This was clearly a one time thing. Sure he was caring, handsome and funny, but he was also an assassin.

Even that's a little hot. I slapped myself again. *No it's not.*

I walked over to Te'ryn's crate, focusing on the contents. Blasters, knives, my blue body paint and grenades? He was extremely prepared to fight. Te'ryn stepped into the room, now with pants on, his muscled chest covered with old scars left exposed to the elements.

"Sorry, I know you said hands off, but I think it's only fair I get something to defend myself with," I said without turning.

Te'ryn pulled a dagger from the chest, holding it with the hilt towards me. "Everything I own is yours, Val."

My eyes widened and my smile spread. "Damn, I should've slept with you earlier if I knew this is how it was going to be."

"Do you know how much it costs to sleep with a human? You just saved me a ton of credits." He returned my smirk.

I kicked his shin. He fell to the ground pulling his shin to his chest. "Ah no! Guess I'll have to go with no legs after all." He peeked through one eye, checking my reaction.

I rolled my eyes, turning my attention back

to the dagger in my hand. "What's the plan to fix the ship?"

Te'ryn sat down next to me disassembling a blaster. "We'll scavenge the old mining equipment, and take what we need to make a makeshift wing." He inspected the barrel, running a cloth through it.

"And you think we'll last long enough? Can't you send out a message to a friend or something?"

He stopped cleaning the blaster, and stared at me. "Unfortunately you're the only friend I have, and your friends would make things messy."

"I know, I don't think I could get you to play nice."

"It's hard to play nice with someone who wants you in chains, unless it's in bed, that is." He leaned forward, pressing a quick kiss to my lips.

I opened my mouth to speak, but closed it. Te'ryn had a point. J'tan and the team would not miss the opportunity to turn Te'ryn in, and I would lose my opportunity to earn all those credits. *Plus, how could I send him to prison?*

"Fine," I sighed. "But if your plan fails, I'll put you back on my kick-ass list."

"I would expect no less."

He reached into his jacket pocket for the

blue stone and placed the gem in my palm. "Hold on to this for me."

The *Heart of the Renari* was rumored to give new emperors the wisdom to rule, but it just looked like a dull blue rock. I nodded and Te'ryn slipped the stone back into my pocket. I was now closer than ever to getting back to Earth. My heart swelled at the thought of seeing my friends, planet and even that crappy diner back home. I couldn't wait to eat pancakes till I got sick. My thoughts turned to my crew—J'tan, Avi, Evi and now Te'ryn, they were the only good things about this side of the universe. My chest tightened at the thought of having to say goodbye sooner than I planned. I was going to miss all of them, even Te'ryn. *Only a tiny bit though.*

"So what does a *front-end-developer* do exactly?" Te'ryn kept his eyes lowered, focused on his already cleaned blaster.

"Uh…I make virtual displays for a business that sells machines for peoples homes," I said, not sure how to explain it to an alien. I had tried my hand at working on alien software but it was much more complex than I could comprehend.

Te'ryn let out a snort as he stood and made his way out of the bunker. I watched through a small dusty window as Te'ryn walked over to the old digging machine. He started to shoot at it, firing at one of the claws till it hung precariously from the blaster-shredded metal arm. With a kick, he freed it from the machine. He hauled it to the ship, a trail of dust made in his wake. Even from where I stood I could see his muscles flexing with each pull. He stopped shortly in front of the ship, dropping the claw to the ground. He ran his hand through his hair, standing with his hand resting on his hip cocked —in a very human manner.

I stifled my laugh, not wanting Te'ryn to hear. I was getting sentimental too soon. *We're going to be here a long time.*

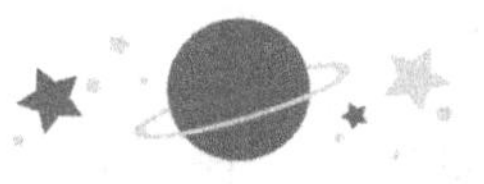

TWENTY-FOUR

Star System 54

TE'RYN

I awoke from slumber to the unmistakable rumble of engines. Val stirred beside me, slowly sitting up.

"Is it the Renari?" She asked, rubbing her eyes.

"I'm not sure—grab a blaster and stay hidden." I swept a piece of hair behind her ear and quickly focused on getting dressed.

"There's no way you're taking on a whole ship by yourself, I'll create a distraction or something," she said, standing up from bed.

She blindly searched for her clothing, patting the floor and cursing. I had half a mind to hide them to keep her inside, but she was right; I would need the backup. I handed her the shirt and she put it on, then slid into my too-large boots.

"I'll head over to the ship and wait for your

distraction, then I'll take out the pilot. Looks like we found our way home." I gave her a smile that she couldn't see. "Also try not to get killed." I meant it this time, I had just found Val again and there was no way I would lose her now.

"Worry about yourself," she said, her voice a little shaky and her brows pinched.

Ah, so she does care. I held down a chuckle. She tried so hard to keep up her stoic front, but it never held up. I lured her in for another kiss and made my way to the entrance.

Pushing the door open a crack, I checked my surroundings. The ship hadn't landed in front of the entrance, putting me more at a disadvantage. Val stood behind me, blaster ready and a wary look on her face. I gave her a human nod, and took slow steps out of the bunker. Keeping my back to the wall, I shuffled to the other side. A large silver Basillian carrier descended towards the gray earth.

It can't be. I waited to see if my suspicions proved true. After the dust settled, the door to the carrier slid open. Several suited Basillians made their way down the ramp, each with a blaster in hand. Following behind them a Basillian dressed in familiar Amaxian silks emerged. It stopped at the top of the ramp, taking in its surroundings. I cursed under my breath, the Basillians must have put a tracker on me. I counted the guards. There were only six,

Val and I would have a chance. *I'll just have to take care of the pilot and disable the carrier's cannons first.*

As the guards marched towards my destroyed ship, I started in the direction of the carrier. I made a large circle, keeping out of sight. Nearing the ship, I crouched down. One careful step after another led me to the entrance. The client hadn't moved from his spot and stood with his back to the ship about six *div* away.

I need a distraction.

Almost as though Val had heard my thoughts, an explosion from the bunker shook the ground beneath me. *She must have found the grenades.* Leaving no time to think, I leapt up the ramp, rushing inside the ship. The contrast between the murky heat of the ship and the cold planet caused my lungs to contract. I steadied my breath listening to the sounds of blaster shots echoing from outside.

Hang in there, Val.

I carried on through the sweltering corridors. Making it to the bridge, I pulled my dagger free from its sheath. I hit the panel to open the door and readied myself. A lone figure cloaked in black stood amidst the empty pilot chairs.

"They assumed this would be your plan," the figure said in Alderian.

"They must not have much faith in my

abilities if they just left you," I scoffed, my arm raised.

Quick as lightning, he flew towards me. His dagger clashed with mine, forcing me back a step. *He's strong.* I pushed forward against his advances, parrying each swing. As the figure took another step back, I whipped a throwing dagger out, sending it flying towards him. His reflexes shot his arm up, knocking the dagger off its trajectory—leaving him wide open. I swung my dagger down, catching him in the shoulder before he could react. Not letting the pain slow him down, he came at me with another flurry of blows.

His moves were getting predictable. He swung wide, and I caught his wrist, twisting downwards till he released his grasp on the dagger. The dagger fell to the ground with a *clank*, and I kicked it out of reach.

"I didn't get this far by pretending to swing a dagger around," I said, knocking his feet out from beneath him.

Still holding his twisted arm, I bent down, running my dagger along his neck. As I began to apply pressure to the blade, the sound of the doors opening behind me caused me to stop.

"I should have known he wouldn't be worth the money. Kill him if you want," the Basillian client said with a note of disdain in its voice.

"If you knew that, then why even try? I was

planning on getting the *Heart* to you, but it seems you're not keen on keeping the deal." I turned my head, gaze pinned on the Basillian.

"Yes well, I was planning on coming to a compromise with you, but it looks like I might have something you want to trade for." The Basillian motioned out into the hall, and a guard stomped into the room, pulling Val behind it.

It was difficult to keep my emotions down. Anger blazing, I released the figure on the ground and charged towards the Basillian.

"Hold on, this one is more valuable alive, is she not?" The Basillian said as the guard pushed its blaster against her head, causing her neck to crane at an uncomfortable angle.

I skid to a stop. "I'll give you the *Heart*, just let her go."

A toothy grin stretched across its textured face. "That's hardly a trade, as I currently have both in my possession."

The Basillian pulled the *Heart of the Renari* from Val's pocket, her face pale. As she turned to look at me, her eyes widened.

"Te'ryn watch out!" She screamed, as a dagger plunged through my heart.

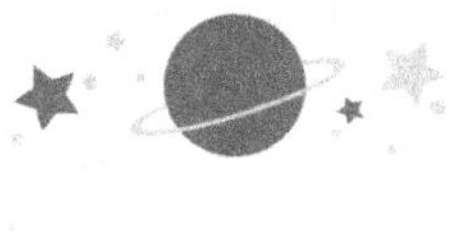

TWENTY-FIVE

Star System 54

VAL

The ugly frog looking guards had to drag me away from the bridge. Kicking and screaming, I thrashed against their hold.

"Te'ryn!" I screamed.

I could no longer see him from the hall. I had helplessly watched as the cloaked figure stabbed him through the heart. The sound of my heart pounded in my ears, and sweat dripped down my brow. *Please be alive, please have some weird alien magic,* I begged the heartless gods of my planet. The guards dragged me through the humid hallway. My hair was plastered to my face, making it difficult to see through the curtains of brown. After several moments, the guards came to a stop at a small door at the end of the corridor.

As one guard released my arm to open the door, I pulled the hidden dagger free, swinging it towards their back. The guard turned and caught my hand with a sick *crunch*. I dropped the dagger. Ignoring the pain, I swung my leg. As my shin collided with the stocky guard, a sharp pain exploded from the point of impact. The guard's large black eyes flicked towards me, then back to the door, completely unfazed. I crumpled to the floor, the guard's hand around my arm being the only thing holding me up. As the other guard forced the door open, the one with their grip on me swung their arm, throwing me effortlessly into the room. I fell to the ground, catching myself on my hands and knees, pain shooting through my body.

"Careful, humans sell for a lot, we don't want her damaged," I heard a croaky voice say as the doors slid shut.

I limped over to the door. I threw my fist against the metal, ignoring the jolt of pain with each hit.

"Te'ryn!" I yelled.

After several more useless hits, I slumped to the ground. I was back where I started.

Helpless and weak.

The ship's engines rattled the metal beneath me, and for the first time in a year, I let myself truly cry.

"SHE'S NOT EATING ANYTHING," I heard a guard say as they removed a tray full of untouched food. I laid on the ground unmoving, not even sparing my captors a look.

"No matter, we'll reach Grihan soon. It will be their problem then." The guards shuffled away, the small room returning to silence.

I could've skipped several steps and ended up where I was going. What did I even try for? Te'ryn's wicked smile came to mind and I attempted to hold back tears. I'd spent the last several days replaying the scene of him being stabbed, his dark blood spilling everywhere, in my head over and over.

Maybe if I had…

I stopped myself. I had gone over every single scenario but it was too late. I could do nothing now. I closed my eyes waiting for sleep to fall over me, giving me a short rest from my thoughts.

Some time later, I was shaken awake as a Basillian hauled me off the floor. Limping, I followed them down the ramp outside. I blinked as bright light hit my eyes and a cool breeze hit my face——a welcome feeling from the days spent in the sweltering heat of the ship. I took a look at my surroundings. Ships of all sizes sat docked along golden cliffs topped with multicolored grasses that sprawled across rolling hills. If I didn't feel so sick to my stomach, I might have enjoyed the view.

The guard nudged me forward and we made our way up a cobblestone pathway lit up with holograms directing foot traffic from glider traffic. Lining the streets, multi-colored houses and shops sat nestled together. Vendors peddled their wares, calling out to the streets bustling with patrons. The smell of spices and fresh food wafted everywhere, causing my empty stomach to rumble. I felt cheated. I had spent so long running from this place, and it was like something out of a painting.

The least they could do is make it look like shit. We continued onward, aliens stopping to stare at the new human being paraded through the street. Conversations in all languages filled the crowd around me.

I didn't have enough time to hear what was being said, because the Basillian pushed me through a large gate. On the other side, the strong smell of florals filled my nose. A tall fountain sat in the center of a courtyard, surrounded by exotic plants of all sizes and colors. More surprisingly, there were several human women and men, dressed in jewel tone robes chatting amongst the flowers. Noticing my arrival, they all turned to watch as the Basillian prodded me forward through the open arches into the building.

We pressed on through the arched hallways, humans watching with interest each time I passed a new group. *How many are there?* I wondered as we passed another group that hushed their talking as soon as we came into view. We soon arrived at a pair of large doors made out of shimmering burgundy wood.

"As she is part of my original stock, I can't offer you more than thirty-thousand credits," I heard a female Jaxian voice say.

"I can certainly get more than that from other parties, so I will have to take my business elsewhere," said the croaky voice of the Basillian, the one who had ordered the cloaked figure to stab Te'ryn.

I clenched my fists. The guard pushed the double doors open, causing the conversation to pause. Inside a small ornate office stood a female Jaxian. She was dressed in a deep red robe, with bangles decorating her arms and tail, watching attentively as we entered the room. She took slow steps towards us, her bangles jingling softly. Reaching a finger out and propping my chin up, she spoke. "You want more for her? She's been damaged." She ran one of her sharp nails down my neck.

Her golden eyes scrutinized me as she took in a whiff.

"I can assure you she is fine. All she needs is

a couple shots of *Relarth*," the Basillian continued, gesturing to me.

"And the Alderian I smell on her?"

"Dead."

My head jolted to the side, eyes burning. *There's no way Te'ryn is dead, he took down a whole ship of Renari guards, a knife should be nothing to him.*

The Jaxian let out a sigh and turned back towards the Basillian. "Two-hundred-thousand, not a credit more."

"That is…acceptable. Thank you for your business." The Basillian stood up and gave her a slight bow. It walked out through the archway giving me a wide grin as it passed.

"You fucking bastard! I'll kill you!" I sprung at it.

Before I could take a step, I felt the strong hands of the Basillian guard wrap around my neck, pushing me to the floor. I landed on my bad leg, letting out a hiss of pain.

The Jaxian tsk-tsked under her breath as she stepped around to face me. "This is a house of new beginnings, you're lucky to be here. I saved you from your disease ridden planet, and here you'll be worshiped by the males around you."

I opened my mouth to speak, but choked as I felt a searing pain from a golden bracelet she wrapped around my wrist. I fell to my knees gasping and clawing at the painful thing.

"You'll come to be grateful for this

opportunity, but this is to assure you behave. Try not to make me use it often." Her tail swished as she opened the side door of the small office.

"Jordan, come help her get situated," she called out.

The burning pain let up, and I was able to breathe again. A tall thin woman with long black hair and brown eyes bent down to look at me.

"Let's go." She glanced at the Jaxian then to me.

I took a wobbly step. She wrapped an arm around my shoulders leading me out of the office and down the arched corridor.

"This is the courtyard, everyone is allowed here in the evening. In the morning, it's just for us humans." Jordan broke the silence.

I gave her a slight nod, not paying attention to my surroundings. "This is the cafeteria—are you even paying attention?" Jordan stopped, crossing her arms and pursing her lips.

"I- sorry I just..." I was speaking in Alderian. I switched back to English, the hard consonants feeling foreign on my tongue. "It's been a long day," I said, not meeting her gaze.

Her eyes softened and she released her tense shoulders. "I get it, we've all been there. But this is important and you might not get a second chance. Bolxi doesn't like us wasting time when we can be earning money."

"I take it that entertaining guests is the way to make money?" I asked the obvious as I tried to take in my surroundings more, heeding Jordan's warning.

"Well, there's what you're thinking of, but there's other ways too. As long as you pay Bolxi the monthly fee, she doesn't care much where it comes from."

Jordan paused in front of a single wooden door. She pushed it open, leading into a large room with open arched walls. Beyond the arches sat the scenery of rolling hills—reds, yellows and greens blending together to make a breathtaking scene. A light breeze fluttered throughout the room, occasionally rustling the vibrant red curtains that lined the arches. A large sunken seating area furnished the room, as well as an ornate table set with a vase full of deep purple flowers. It was stunning, everything on this planet was. And for some reason it made me angrier.

"This is your room, guests are allowed in as long as you welcome them. Bolxi is serious about our safety, so if someone gets too aggressive, or wants something more than you want to give, you can call security over here." Jordan ran her hand down a panel, displaying options in English. "The prices to charge for talking, eating a meal etc. can be found here too." She pointed out the costs for each action.

Eye contact: twenty credits. I snorted after reading that section.

"You laugh now but it adds up. Those Alderians love our eye colors, since they only have silver," Jordan said, closing the tablet. "Anyways, you look like hell, take a bath and I'll be back later to finish the tour." She removed her hand from the panel and left the room.

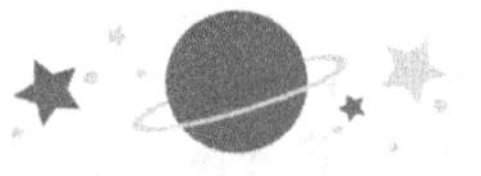

TWENTY-SIX

Star System 86

VAL

The hot water was magic to my sore muscles. I watched as my blood from my old wounds turned the water a slight pink. My shin now sported a large black and blue bruise. *Jordan is right, I probably do look like hell.* I waited till the water turned cold before emerging from the bath. I made my way over to the small vanity stocked with various perfumes, salves and hair products. Catching my reflection in the mirror, I noticed the dark bags below my eyes. Bruises and cuts speckled my body.

Bolxi wasted her money on me.

I swept the contents of the vanity onto the floor, glass shattering on the multi-colored tiles. It felt good to break something. To make this awful perfect place feel less pristine. Being abducted, then being thrust into a new world and even my break up with Robert hadn't made me feel this terrible. Robert and I had been together nearly a decade. With the break up I had lost all our shared friends, my apartment and dog. We had grown into different people and it hurt to separate, but it didn't hurt as bad as losing Te'ryn.

I walked over the shards of glass, reveling in the pain from the pricks in my bare feet. I felt like I deserved the pain, like my body finally hurt as much as my heart. As I reached for the vase of flowers, Jordan stepped into the room.

"Really? You're going to have to pay for that. Acting like a spoiled child," she said, taking in the mess around the room.

A woman with short curly hair stepped around her. "Jordan, you have no place to talk, you threw a bed out the second story-" she stopped as I met her familiar face. It was Lynn from the Azzek ship. "Val. You're alive?"

She ran towards me. Jordan grabbed her arm, stopping her before she could step on glass.

"We thought for sure you were dead. What happened, why are you here now?" She spoke a mile a minute.

"Hold on, hold on." Jordan threw her arms up between us.

"Lynn, you can ask her a million questions later, we need to get her checked out by the doctor." She turned to me, eyes clearly avoiding my lack of clothes.

"Val, please get dressed. Once we get you healed up you can break as many vases as you can pay for."

Suddenly feeling embarrassed, I stepped cautiously around the glass shards using my good leg, the pain coming back in full force. I fell into a chair near the bath, pulling the robe off the hanger. I limped back to Jordan, now fully dressed.

"Good. Now that we got that covered, let's go," Jordan said as Lynn put her arm around me, helping me walk.

"Nice pun," Lynn whispered and Jordan let out a snort.

We followed the twisting corridors till we reached the med bay. The equipment was similar to what I'd seen on other ships, but instead of the sterile white I was used to, this room was decorated with colorful murals depicting the hills of Grihan. As we stepped into the room, a shorter-than-average Alderian looked up from his desk, scattered papers falling to the floor. His tousled black hair shook as he adjusted his spectacles.

"Lynn, did you get in another fight?" He asked in accented English.

"No, take off those stupid glasses so you can see right, Ke'dan," Lynn said, a note of anger in her voice.

He removed the thick glasses, blinking as his

eyes adjusted. When his eyes passed over me, his eyebrows shot up. "Oh, bring her over here," he pointed to the exam table. Lynn and Jordan helped me up onto the table. "What happened?" He fiddled with vials of liquid on a counter.

"She was redecorating. Not a fan of Bolxi's style," Jordan retorted.

"Ah, you weren't either, Jordan, if I remember correctly." He gave her a wink as he continued mixing the liquid till it turned a bright purple.

"It was one time." She rolled her eyes as Ke'dan moved her out of the way with a gentle nudge of his hand. He began examining my bloody feet. "It'll just be a quick shot-"

"I know, I've had *Relarth* before," I answered in Alderian. Ke'dan's eyebrow twitched at the use of his language. He bent down, and started to administer the *Relarth*. As I watched Ke'dan inject the liquid, I remembered the other time I had gotten a shot of the stuff. Evi had gotten a bit too invested in sparring and broke my arm during a throw. It took three bottles of the stuff to get it healed and it was months before Evi sparred with me again. I hoped she and the rest of J'tan's team were okay, I hadn't been able to contact them since I had stowed away on Te'ryn's ship.

I felt the burn of my skin knitting back together, focusing on the murals till the pain passed. Ke'dan's silver eyes met mine and I felt a pang of sadness. *Te'ryn, please be okay.* I held back tears.

"Anywhere else you're injured?" Ke'dan asked as he set the empty vial back on the counter.

"She's got nasty gashes on her thigh, hand and shoulder," Lynn interjected before I could reply. Ke'dan mixed up more vials.

"If it's okay, could you show me those wounds?" He walked over, ready with another shot. He first took a look at my hand where the embedded device was visibly destroyed by the tussle with the Basillian. "We'll have to take this out, let's fix the other wounds first."

"Any chance I can get another one?" I asked, hopeful.

"Not here." He shook his head in a human-like gesture. *Of course.* I lamented internally. He moved on to my next injury. After the wound on my thigh healed up, he waited with another vial as I pulled down the collar exposing the last injury. He glanced over it quickly, then froze as he looked at the hologram displaying my body scan.

"What, that bad?" I forced an awkward laugh. Te'ryn had tried his best to wrap it up.

"Hold on, you'll just go numb for a second."

I felt my muscles relax. Tingles filled my hands and feet and I couldn't move. Getting nervous, I watched as Ke'dan retrieved the translator from my ear. "This has a tracker in it. *Vaat*, they should have checked you for that first."

He threw the small metal ring into a vial. The liquid fizzed around the metal until it disintegrated.

I had more questions for Te'ryn but those would have to wait. Ke'dan quickly worked on my hand, removing the palmpad. My heart sank. The crew had worked several missions to pay for that. Unable to speak, I waited.

"Well, you won't need that since your friend is dead. The numbing agent should be wearing off now."

"He's not fucking dead!" I snapped, raising my voice as soon as I was able.

Lynn set her hands on my shoulders and faced Ke'dan.

"How about we give her some time? She just got here and needs some time to adjust."

He sighed and slid his hands into his pockets. "Alright, but help her adjust *fast*. You know how Bolxi is." He turned, focusing his attention back on his cluttered desk, only giving us a slight wave as we turned to leave.

"And that was Ke'dan," Jordan said under her breath after we exited the room.

"Don't get too cozy with him, he acts nice

but he's a kiss ass to Bolxi," Lynn added, leading the way through the maze of hallways.

As we walked back to the room—my room now, I started piecing together a plan to escape. *Te'ryn better not be dead, because I'm going to be the one that gets to kill him.*

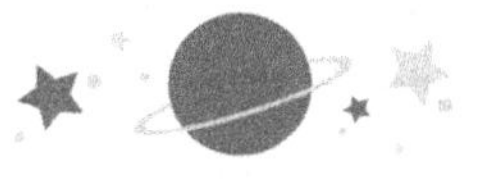

Star System 86

VAL

Lynn and Jordan left me to myself for the rest of the evening. After they had finished their tour of the pleasure house, they went back to work, giving me the tentative start date of tomorrow. I paced my room as the sun set, the building's lamps filling the darkness with vibrant yellows and reds. Talking, laughing and all sorts of bustle from the incoming crowd reverberated around me. Echoes of passion filled the halls outside my room. Waiting till the sound of footsteps passed, I opened the door a crack, peeking into the outside hall. The bracelet around my wrist was one problem, figuring out the security around the building was another.

Going the opposite way of the noise, I set off towards the cafeteria. Food then reconnaissance. I would need to regain my strength. Careful to avoid notice, I stepped into a small alcove as I heard the sound of footsteps approaching. A hushed voice spoke, and I recognized it as Lynn.

"I don't think I'm going to make enough this month, Bolxi is going to auction me off." The desperation was evident in her tone.

"Don't worry, I'll take on some more clients. You'll be okay," Jordan replied warmly.

"I hate when you do that," Lynn sniffed. Soft sounds of kisses filled the silence.

"Come on, we better get back to it," Lynn sighed.

I stepped further back into the shadows in the alcove, not wanting to be caught listening to such a private moment. They passed by, arms entangled in each other, unaware of my presence. I let out a breath and continued on my way, sympathetic for the trapped couple.

Worry about yourself, Val. I repeated my mantra.

If I was going to get out I would have to do it covertly—alone. I entered the cafeteria and froze after noticing the crowd. Alderians and a few other species mingled with humans over food. The smell of the freshly cooked meals made my mouth water. It had been days since I last ate anything that wasn't sand or re-hydrated. I stayed close to the wall, eyes locked on a table stacked with an assortment of pastries made with various fruits.

While passing behind a group of Alderians,

one dressed in black silks with his silver hair plaited into a long braid, stepped backwards, accidentally bumping into me.

"Ah sorr-" He stopped speaking in Alderian when he saw me. "Hey, how do you say sorry in Human?" He turned to his friend, looking annoyed.

"You didn't download the language?" His friend laughed and slapped him on the shoulder, the other two joining in the jests.

"Don't worry about it," I mumbled in Alderian and stepped around him. His hand caught my wrist, twisting me back around.

"Hold on, let's talk more. I haven't seen you before," he said, a too-wide smile stretching across his face.

His friends now watched me, eyes focused like a predator targeting its prey.

"That's because you can't afford me, honey." I emphasized the words, removing his hand from my wrist. I felt the hard metal beneath his palm, giving me an idea.

If I can get access to one of the aliens' palmpads, then I could contact my crew and secure a way off the planet. But that would come after getting my hands on some of those delicious pastries. His friends laughed at my comment, causing his ears to turn a dark blue. Not giving him a chance to retort, I skirted in between the crowd, making it to the food table.

I stacked up as many pastries as possible onto a small opalescent plate. I shoved an extra one into my mouth for good measure. Turning, my eyes locked on the Alderian who grabbed me earlier, now making his way through the crowd towards me. Securing my bounty, I hurried off the opposite way, ducking and squeezing between the large aliens. Careful not to make eye contact, I ignored more calls for my attention around me. After safely making it out to the hallway, I shoved another pastry into my mouth. I let out a soft moan. This place was worse than the pit of hell, but they sure made good pastries.

"Hey, wait." A voice from behind stopped me from taking another bite. I turned around slowly, hoping it wasn't the Alderian I insulted earlier. A slim Alderian with white hair pulled up into a ponytail, wearing burnt orange robes, walked towards me. *Oh great, it's his friend.*

"Va'lr may not be able to afford your company, but I certainly can." His grin was full of confidence and his shoulders were square, with an air about him that made it seem like he was certain he would get what he wanted. *Someone to take advantage of.*

I returned his words with my cheesiest smile. "Unfortunately I am off for tonight, but if you're here tomorrow..." I fluttered my eyelashes at him for extra effect. It worked. His grin grew wider and he stepped towards me, his hand brushing through my hair. He brought a lock of my hair to his lips and kissed it.

"For you, I would stay several rotations." He left, returning to the cafeteria.

Maybe if I hadn't met Te'ryn I would have thought him handsome, but it was difficult to look at any Alderian the same after. I pushed the pang of sadness away, I had to focus on getting out first. Then I could find Te'ryn. I took a bite of the pastry in my hand, trying to shake the bad taste in my mouth.

"Nice one, you'll fit in swimmingly."

I looked for the origin of the voice, growing agitated at all the obstacles between me and my food. I spotted a pair of checkered Vans peeking out beneath black silks.

"Sara. It's good to see you again."

"You know, I saw you that day. When you escaped after the explosion." She crossed her arms. I gulped down the rest of my pastry and looked at the floor, trying to come up with an explanation.

"Don't even pretend you feel guilty, you know any of us would have done the same. I had hoped you made it away and were living a better life, but it looks like you just ended up in the same shit hole as the rest of us."

'Sara I-" I stopped, there was nothing I could say. I did leave them back on that space station, and nothing I said could change that. But I had been given a second chance—a chance to finally help them. *Am I willing to help them even if it risks my plan failing?*

"Was it nice at least? Out there?" Her voice softened.

"It was."

"Good, at least it was worth it." She straightened herself up, turning to leave after she had said everything she meant to.

I stepped in front of her.

Yes. I'm going to help them.

I decided. No matter what happened, I would not regret trying. "Let me make it up to you. Give me a day." I held her gaze for a moment.

"It'd better be good," she said with a snort, as she continued on her path.

I made my way back to my room, determined to help more than just myself.

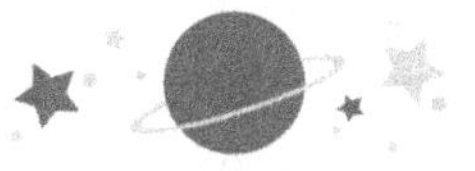

TWENTY-EIGHT

Star System 86

VAL

The morning light filtered through the open arches, giving the room a much colder appearance than the evening before. In the deep set seating area, Sara, Jordan and Lynn sat eagerly awaiting for me to speak.

"Are Marie and Logan not coming?" I looked at Sara.

"Marie ran off with some Alderian she claimed to be her mate," Sara said, clearly not shaken by the impressive feat.

"And Logan?"

Sara shrugged.

I hoped Marie was happy wherever she was. Being a human on this side of the universe made life difficult, I could only hope her mate was ready to take on everything that came along with that. I was not surprised about Logan. I could understand he didn't want to take any more risks after settling here, but I couldn't help being worried that he might let our plans slip.

"Yeah, with Marie running away and another client being assassinated, security has gotten crazy strict," Lynn added, making it sound as uneventful as rain in the forecast.

"Yeah one of us just had to fall for a good looking doctor—oh wait—assassin," Sara said, her anger focused on Jordan.

"Look, he just paid me to talk and drink, it was a good deal." Jordan folded her arms.

This is sounding too familiar. "Woah woah woah, was this doctor-assasin's name Fet'lan by any chance?" I asked.

Jordan's eyes widened. "The very one, how did you know?"

Of course it was Te'ryn. He had mentioned visiting Grihan before. Somehow he managed to make things more difficult for me even before we met. I was curious if he was honest about what happened with Jordan, but I didn't have the heart to ask.

"Long story short, I was working as a bounty hunter. That's why I called you all here. If I can get a hold of a palmpad, I can reach out to my crewmates and they can help us get off this planet."

"You were a bounty hunter? Sick," Sara said. It was the first time I'd ever heard her slightly interested in anything.

"I think you're forgetting the bracelet around your wrist. If you leave you'll be wishing you were dead." Jordan gestured to the gold ring.

I was the only one wearing one, meaning they had all earned Bolxi's trust. I continued speaking. "I'm sure my crewmates will be able to help with that, I just need to reach them first. I agreed to let some pompous Alderian visit me tonight, so all I need is something to knock him out with."

"Let's say we believe your crew will come. Why would we leave here just to be stuck on some shitty-ass planet? At least we have food and safety here." Jordan stood to her full height, she was at least five inches taller than me. Even though she was shorter than the aliens I usually dealt with, her posture and scowl made me feel particularly small.

I pulled the *Heart of the Renari* out of the flower pot I stashed it in shortly after arriving here. I'd kept it hidden in my clothing and the Basillians hadn't even thought to check that their *Heart of the Renari* was the real one. "This will sell for at least a couple hundred-thousand credits. It should give us plenty to buy a trip back home to Earth."

"I'm in. I'll do anything to get out of here," Sara said.

"Me too," Lynn added, a determined look upon her face.

Jordan's head whipped around, not believing that Lynn had agreed with my plan. "Lynn you can't, we don't know if her plan will work. If it fails, we'll all be punished."

"Jordan, you know I won't last long here, I barely scrape by each month even with your help," Lynn replied, keeping her posture strong.

Jordan held her gaze for a while, then relaxed her shoulders in defeat, letting out a sigh. "I guess that means I'm in too."

Now that I had everyone on board with my plan, the weight of responsibility hit me. I had to succeed. I knew J'tan, Avi and Evi would have my back, but it didn't make me feel any less nervous.

We spent the next hour discussing plans and Lynn volunteered to get sleeping pills from Ke'dan. She had already been taking them, so asking for more wouldn't be too suspicious. The only thing left to do was wait for my guest to show up. Jordan helped me with my hair, hiding the valuable stone within the many braids. She was reluctant to talk, only answering with yes or no. I knew she wasn't entirely on board but she wouldn't go anywhere without Lynn. After fixing my hair, Jordan left in order to keep up appearances.

Later in the afternoon, I heard a soft knock on my door. I opened it, expecting one of the other women to be back. Instead I found Logan standing there, looking better than I'd ever seen him. The color had returned to his tan skin and he stood tall draped in red silks, looking like a greek statue with his grown out curly black hair.

"Can I come in?" He asked softly.

"Oh, um yeah." I stepped out of the way, allowing him to enter.

He looked around cautiously then spoke in a low voice. "Whatever you're thinking, it's not a good idea. Bolxi has this place locked down tight."

"No one is making you come. Just stay out of it if that's what you want. If you say anything, I swear you'll regret it." I was hardly intimidating to someone as large as Logan, but everything was riding on this opportunity. I would use as many threats as I could.

"I was just warning you. That's all." He grabbed the door handle, preparing to leave. "If you're smart, you'll listen before you have to learn the hard way."

I watched as he left, anxiety kicking in. I paced the room thinking of everything that could go wrong, only stopping when the golden light of the setting suns filled the room returning it to its ethereal glow. I heard a knock at the door, and suddenly the pastries I had for dinner weren't sitting too well in my stomach. I walked over slowly, steading my breath. *Just talk, then get him to drink.* I opened the door, the Alderian wasted no time entering.

He strode in, each step full of confidence, then flung himself on the couch resting a leg on the coffee table.

"Um, hello," I said, surprised at how quickly he made himself at home.

"You look ravishing tonight, why don't you join me down here?" His tongue slid across his lips.

Clenching my jaw, I forced my lips into a tight smile. I knew he was going to be a hassle, but he was turning out to be more of an ass than I expected. I grabbed the drinks from the table, making sure to check the small black mark on the glass, noting it was the one full of the liquified sleeping pills.

I sat near him, keeping a pillow in between us, as if it was a wall. I handed him the drink. "So tell me about yourself, I have to admit I don't know anything about you."

I took a sip of my drink, watching the glass in his hand with intense concentration. He raised it to his lips, not drinking, and lowered it before he spoke. "Other than I'm incredibly handsome, you mean. And rich, look at these silks I spent thousands of credits on."

He swished the black fabric, causing ripples of blue and green to spread across the fabric. *Oh my god, just drink!* I screamed internally as I kept a smile plastered to my face half-listening to him talk about the qualities of Amaxian silk.

"Fascinating," I said, trying to make sure he didn't notice my eyes glaze over.

"It is isn't it, but let's not talk about me. I want to hear about you."

"Oh there's not much to talk about. Is the drink not to your liking? I can get you another one." The less he knew about me the better.

"I do like Korop, it's just that I like it much better when it's not spiked with something." He swirled his glass then flashed me a devilish grin.

My heart felt stuck in my throat. My mind raced thinking of things to say. Instead of speaking, I jolted up, ready to rush to the door. *How did he find out, did someone rat me out?* Before I took a step, I felt the Alderian's strong grasp around my wrist.

"Oh seriously Val, how could I not know there was something in it when you wear every emotion on your face." He pulled me closer.

My training kicked in and I twisted under his arm, throwing my weight forward. It threw him off balance for a second, but that was all I needed. I curled forward, flipping him over me and onto his back.

I'll just knock him out the hard way then. He let out a puff of air then kicked back up to standing quicker than I expected. His leg shot out, catching me in the crook of my knee, sending me to the ground. A hilt of a dagger strapped to his thigh glinted in the light from the shuffling of his silks. As he reached down to pin my arms, I freed the dagger bringing it to his neck.

"Well this is not the hospitality I paid for, but I do have a thing for bad girls." His smile widened.

"Well it's too bad I don't like spoiled rich boys," I said, my breathing heavy from the fight.

"Oh not into rich boys huh? How about a particular assassin?" He tapped his neck, and the face of the spoiled Alderian melted into the face of Te'ryn still smiling at me with that stupid mischievous look of his.

"I'm going to fucking kill you." Tears streamed down my cheeks. I dropped the dagger and wrapped my arms around his neck.

"Do you want me dead or alive? I'm getting mixed signals here." He chuckled as he pulled me in closer.

"If you die, I'll bring you back to life and kill you myself."

"You're the only one I'd let kill me." Te'ryn held my face in his hands, wiping the tears off my cheeks.

All the stress from the last couple of days melted away in Te'ryn's arms. I didn't feel so alone anymore. He helped me up from the floor. Sitting on the couch, he lifted me onto his lap, his face close enough to feel his breath. "Did you like my act?"

"It was too good, I was ready to fall asleep after your explanation." I smacked his chest gently. Taking in his brilliant silver eyes, I realized exactly how much I had missed them these last couple days.

His lips gently brushed my forehead and then my lips. I leaned forward hungry for more, but he lightly pushed my face back with his hands. He ran his thumb along the gold rings around my wrist. "So tell me, what was your escape plan this time?"

TWENTY-NINE

Star System 54

TE'RYN

Days earlier

"Vaat." I groaned as my back hit the ground, dust flying everywhere as the carrier took off. I had failed Val when I promised I would protect her. My blood mixed with the soil beneath me. My vision blurred. I would get her back, and when I did, there would be hell to pay for that *vaating* Basillian. I struggled against my waning strength as I moved my hand to my pocket, pulling the earpiece free. I pushed it into my ear, begging the universe it still worked.

"Val, what the *vaat* happened? Why do you have a bounty on your head?" A female voice demanded.

"Gone, she's gone," I said, struggling with each word.

"Who are you? What have you done with Val?" A male voice asked, the anger apparent in his voice.

"I'm on Planet Four-Three-Six-Nine-Two-Zero, I can help you find her." I took in a breath, this one more shallow than the last.

"And why should we trust you?" Another male with a gruff voice asked.

"Because I'm the only chance you got." Darkness filled my view, and I hoped I had said enough.

"EVI, I'm pretty sure that's enough *Relarth*." My head pounded and ears rang as I regained consciousness.

"Shut up Avi, I'm going to give this bastard enough *Relarth* to wake up talking." She stabbed another vial into my gut.

I inhaled sharply.

"I'm talking, I don't think I need anymore," I said, eyes opening from the pain spreading throughout my chest.

Two familiar Undrians and a burly Alderian with a scar across one eye stood over me. I went to move my hand, but halfway it snapped back towards the table. I checked my other appendages, drawing the same conclusion; each was bound to the cool metal table beneath me.

"Then talk. Where is Val?" Avi asked, holding a knife against my neck.

"No use healing me if you're just going to kill me again," I groaned as the knife drew a couple droplets of blood. Humor was probably not the best tactic right now, but I had a hard time turning it off. "She's on Grihan," I said, testing the strength of the bonds.

"No way, we totally didn't guess that," Evi replied, sarcasm dripping from her voice.

I felt another stab in my stomach as the burning sensation of my flesh knitting back together continued.

"You're going to have to make yourself a little more useful if you want to keep from bleeding out," Avi said, wrenching the needle free from my gut.

I let out a groan. They were not going easy on me. "I know where it is, and how to get in." The location of Grihan was a well kept secret. Only those with the coordinates and the code would be able to find and land on the planet without getting blasted apart by sentries.

"Alright, give us the coordinates and we can get this over with," the massive Alderian said, his voice gruff. I needed to convince them that I had to go along. Not only was I close to a one way ticket to the Federation's prison, I owed it to Val to go after her.

"I'm going," I said flatly. I had to help Val, I was the only one who could.

"If you think we're stupid enough to just let you walk-" Evi was cut off by the Alderian.

"Why take the risk for a human?" His gaze was unwavering. He had clearly been through a lot. More than the scars or the way he carried himself, his stoic figure held an air of a male who had been to hell and back.

"Because she would come back for me." I held his stare for what felt like an eternity.

He let out a relenting sigh. His eyes were full of understanding. He released the straps around my wrists and ankles, holding his hand out to me to help me sit up. The Undrians looked at him confused, yet they seemed to respect him enough not to challenge his judgment.

Taking one last sweeping look over me, he set off through the doorway. "Let's get to work then."

Present

Val's face scrunched up in between my hands after I asked her what her plan was. "You only had half a plan again huh?" I rested my forehead against hers.

I was glad to have her back in my arms. Losing her had been more difficult than I could imagine. She'd made her way into my heart quicker than I ever thought was possible.

"No, my plan was to knock out that pompous Alderian and reach my crewmates. Wait, was that you the whole time?"

"No, I was in the dinner hall though. This is for my eyes only," I said, squishing her cheeks as she glared daggers my way. I wished I could hold her like this forever, but we had a plan to get under way. "You dropped this." I slid a communicator into her ear.

Val sat listening, looking perplexed at what her crewmates had to share with her, eventually bursting out with a "I did not fuck the bounty! Why do you both even have a bet about that?"

I laughed until I received a nasty glare from Val, causing me to cover my mouth and force the laughter down. She paced the room as she continued listening—probably being filled in on the plan we'd devised. She listened for a couple moments longer, her eyes lighting up.

"Thank you." She beamed. Val pulled the communicator out of her ear and turned to me. "We have three others that we need to get out of here too."

"That's not part of the plan."

"I know, but J'tan is more of an ask for forgiveness than permission sort of guy."

"I'm guessing I don't get any say in this."

"Nope."

I let out a snort at Val's reply. Stars only knew how either of us got anything done with how stubborn we both were.

The doors burst open, revealing a well dressed Jaxian female with several armed Alderians crowded behind her. They quickly filed into the room, aiming their blasters at Val. My hand reached for my blaster hidden under my robe. Waiting for the opportune moment, my eyes followed each guard.

"Valued patron, please step away from the human. She has broken our rules and our trust, if you come with us we can match you with a much more compliant human." The Jaxian smiled showing her sharp teeth—a perfect business smile.

"I rather like this one though." My grip on her tightened. Val's attention was locked on the blasters pointed her way, but I could feel her fist tighten around the silks on my back.

"You won't like this one after you find out what is in your drink." The Jaxian tilted her head towards the table, sending a guard over. Keeping my breath steady, I watched as he picked up the drink, running a scanner over it.

"It's full of sleeping pills," the guard confirmed.

Val looked at me, the anxiety clear in her eyes. *Just a little longer.* I couldn't act with so many blasters pointed at Val.

The Jaxian let out a laugh closer to a growl. "Bring the others in."

More guards shoved three women through the door. Val took in a breath. *These must be the ones she was talking about.*

"Now if you follow me, we'll handle this *incident.*" The Jaxian kept her gaze on me as the guards pushed the women to their knees. "These three helped conspire with you right?" The Jaxian looked to Val but received no response.

I stood, my hand still on my blaster. "I expect you'll make up for this incident," I said, making sure to sound as pompous as possible.

"I can assure you, you will forget this ever happened." The fake smile was still plastered to her face.

I took several steps towards her, and when I caught the guards moving towards Val in my peripheral, I spun and shot. One guard fell to the ground, and shouts filled the air. Val leapt out of the seating area, catching a distracted guard in the neck with one of my daggers.

"Get him you idiots!" The Jaxian screeched as she backed out through the door. The last two guards shielded her, and began to fire.

I rolled back into the seating pit, Val following after.

"This is not part of the plan!" Val yelled over the sound of the blasters firing.

"No, you made sure your plan ruined mine." I sent another two shots, taking out the last two guards in the room.

"We need to move before more show up." I grabbed Val's hand and helped her out of the pit, taking in the destruction around me. The furniture and walls were destroyed. Fortunately, the three, now very scared, human women sat unharmed near the entrance.

Val ran over to them. "This is Te'ryn and he's going to help us get out of here." She helped untie the bonds from around each wrist.

"No, that's the fucking assassin that killed that senator a year ago," the now familiar human said, glaring at me.

What's her name again?

"Jordan, don't worry he's on our side." Val tried to persuade the now skeptical group. *Ah, Jordan, right.* She was the one I spent all those credits just talking to in order to complete a mission.

"He's the assassin? Hell yeah, I'm more on board now," a female with black hair chimed in.

Shouts echoed down the hallway. Reinforcements were on the way.

"Come or not, but I'm getting Val out of

here." I held on to Val's hand, determined not to lose her again.

"Please, I promise he's here to help," Val begged.

"Ugh fine, but if he tries anything, I'm out," Jordan replied, her eyes flicking between the incoming sounds and me.

The women shuffled behind Val and I as we held our blasters close, checking the hall. Seeing that it was clear, we all made our way to the exit. Pushing our way through the crowd, we made it through to the courtyard. Turning the corner, I slid to a stop, motioning for the women behind me to stay. Three guards patrolled the courtyard, blasters in hand. As groups of Alderians shuffled through, the guards made sure to inspect each and every one. Seeing that they were not the ones they were looking for, they allowed the group to exit.

"I'll lead the guards out of the way. Val, you lead the group through the exit and down to the docks." I leaned in and pressed a kiss to her lips.

"See you there," she replied. A brief moment of concern crossed her face, but she quickly forced it into a look of determination.

I held my blaster up, finger on the trigger.

Bang.

I fired at the nearest guard and set off to create a diversion.

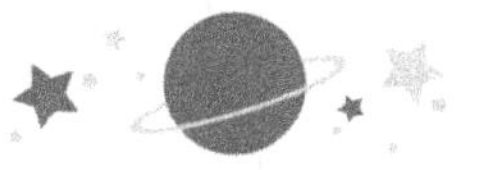

THIRTY

Star System 86

VAL

Te'ryn set off guns blazing—literally, causing enough of a racket to send the whole crowd into a panic. Once the guards ran after Te'ryn, we all rushed into the courtyard forcing our way into the crowd. The chaos of the crowd made it difficult to make a clean break to the entrance. Separated by the bustle of several large aliens, I lost sight of the other women. An elbow met my head and I stumbled, falling deeper into the crowd. I made sure to send my choice curse words towards the male now swallowed by the mass of frightened aliens.

"You little bitch, you set me up."

A strong hand gripped my hair, whipping my head backwards. I struggled against the grip and forced my head to turn to see the assailant. The pompous Alderian Te'ryn had imitated, stood in his underwear firm against the crowd. My hair bunched in his fist.

"Where's my Amaxian silks?" His steel grip pulled me closer causing me to let out a yelp.

"You didn't even come to my room, how would I know?" I said through gritted teeth. I struggled against his hold no no avail.

The Alderian pulled me further from the entrance, pushing through the crowd. "Where's your friend? I know he's around here somewhere."

He dragged me towards a guard who was still in pursuit of Te'ryn. I spun in closer to him, my hands gripping his and I flung my weight forward into a throw the way J'tan had taught me.

The Alderian smacked into the ground onto his back. He held tight to my hair, dragging me to the ground with him. The fall knocked the air out of both of us. I took a breath and swung my arms and legs toward him, feeling the impact of my foot against flesh. Letting out several curses, he released my hair. His eyes met mine, a feral look upon his face. He stood and turned to face me. Before he could approach, a hand spun him around.

"I think I'm the one you're looking for." Te'ryn threw a punch at the Alderian's face, causing him to stumble backward.

I took several steps back, pressing a hand to

my tender scalp, wary of his reach. I watched as Te'ryn sent a kick into his side. The Alderian fell to the ground and curled up into a ball. His motivation to fight was shattered along with his ribs.

Te'ryn wasted no time grabbing my hand as he pulled me back into the crowd. "We need to hurry, my distraction didn't work as well as I hoped."

"That's unusual, you're typically a lot more distracting." I puffed, hoping it could help ease my anxiety.

"Guess they don't know beauty when they see it," Te'ryn said as his head swiveled from left to right watching for any incoming guards.

His hand held fast to mine as we raced through the entrance. Searing pain spread from the ring on my wrist causing my knees to buckle underneath me.

"Val, what's wrong?" Te'ryn's eyes filled with worry as he scanned me looking for the source of my pain.

"Bracelet," I choked out. Elbow locked, I held my wrist away from me as if distance could help alleviate the pain.

"Over here!" Lynn shout-whispered from the alley between two shops. I pushed my leg forward trying to fight through the pain. I forced myself to stand, but it was no use. I fell back down to my hands and knees. Te'ryn lifted me up as if I weighed no more than a bag of feathers, and sprinted to the alleyway.

"What's wrong with her?" Te'ryn growled at the women as if they were the cause of my anguish.

"It's the bracelet. Bolxi puts them on all the new girls so they can't escape," Jordan said, helping Te'ryn set me on the ground.

My breaths became more labored with each moment. The pain moved through my body, making it feel as if my skin was on fire.

"Get it off," I said through clenched teeth.

Te'ryn pulled his black dagger from its sheath. He pushed it against the bracelet with little force. The sound of metal against metal rang through the alley, but the bracelet received only a scratch from the Alderian obsidian.

"Vaat," Te'ryn cursed under his breath. The commands of guards ordering the crowd out of the way sounded closer than ever.

"Just take the other girls please," I begged Te'ryn. I couldn't stand the pain any longer, going back to the pleasure house didn't seem so awful anymore.

"I'm not leaving you, the others be damned." Te'ryn's silver eyes glowed, catching the setting sun's light.

"Ouch." Sara said.

"Then. Cut. It. Off." Every word was

becoming difficult. I didn't know how much longer I could hold on.

"I tried that, it won't come off." He paused, sympathy clear in his face.

"My. Hand." My head fell limp against the wall. Removing a limb seemed the less painful of the two. Te'ryn hesitated for a moment, but ultimately made his decision. He brushed my sweat-plastered hair off my face, then ripped a strip of fabric from his robes, tying it tightly around my arm. "I'll buy you a better hand, I promise." He pressed a kiss against my forehead.

"You better." I let out a small laugh that sounded closer to a sob. I closed my eyes, bracing myself.

"Hell yeah robot hand, just like in Star-" Sara's comment was cut off by my scream of pain.

I wished it was as easy as in the movies, that I could just faint and be done with the suffering. Call it strength or shock but my consciousness held on as the burning pain filling my body moved to my left wrist. My vision swirled, and the sounds around me became muffled as if underwater. The women and Te'ryn argued over something, I couldn't tell what, nor did I care at this point.

The world shifted around me and my stomach threatened to remove all the pastries I had enjoyed earlier. My surroundings rocked back and forth as Te'ryn lifted me. Each movement sent jolts of pain to my wrist.

"Hold on, Val," he said, trying to console me.

Black filled the edges of my vision and I welcomed the darkness.

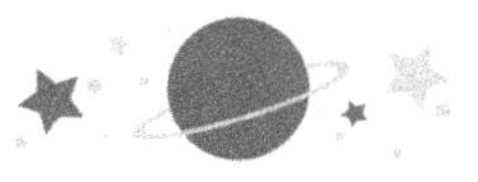

THIRTY-ONE

Star System 86

TE'RYN

Val went limp in my arms. No matter my situation, I'd always remained cool headed. Whether I faced many foes, injury or near death I never worried. Not once. I had always lived on the edge of death; it didn't frighten me. But this…this was different. I felt the panic rise in my chest as I held Val's small body closer.

"We need to go now," I said to the other humans, my patience wearing thin.

I checked around the corner, watching for any incoming guards. The nervous crowd spilled out from the pleasure house in a constant stream. We still had our cover. I motioned to the women to follow. Val would never forgive me if I left them behind.

"Lynn, we need to go back." Jordan's soft voice caught my attention.

I turned around to see Jordan grabbing Lynn by the wrist, trying to lead her back the way we came.

"Jordan you didn't." Lynn's eyes were huge as she shook her head several times.

"You bitch!" Sara spun and slapped Jordan across her face.

Lynn cried, Sara spat several human curse words and Jordan just stood there, stoic as ever.

"I did what I had to do. Bolxi said she would waive your debt for years since I told her. You seriously can't trust *this*." Jordan gestured to me.

"I don't have time for this. If you want to stay, then stay," I growled as I walked towards the crowd.

Sara shot Jordan a nasty look, and followed closely after me. Lynn stood for a moment, not sure what to do. After coming to a conclusion, she finally spoke. "I'm sorry, but I have to go."

Grief filled Jordan's eyes as she grasped Lynn's hand again. "Please, I did what I had to do to keep you safe. We don't know what's out there, Lynn."

"You don't get to make that decision for me!" More tears streamed down her face as she continued speaking. "I'm sure whatever out there is better than this, so I'm going to do what I have to." Lynn tried to free herself from Jordan's grasp.

Warmth spread across my chest and I looked

down to see Val's blood soaking my silks. The hastily made tourniquet was starting to slip. I was running out of time. *I need to get her out of here.* I pulled the blaster free from its holster and pointed it at Jordan.

"We're going now," I said.

Jordan's face blanched as she released Lynn. I sent one last glance her way. Jordan stood behind watching sorrowfully.

I covered Val with the excess silk from my outfit and pushed my way through the hoard of people, hurrying as fast as possible to make it back to the ship. I checked behind me, the women kept close. Good. I would not risk Val going back for them. Luck was on our side as we made it to the docks without incident. The crowd had worked to disguise us. I ran till I spotted J'tan's old ship waiting on the docks and I wasted no time boarding.

The two Undrian twins greeted us in the entrance as the ship moved beneath us, taking off into space. They looked surprised at the appearance of the other two women but their attention quickly turned to the unconscious Val in my arms.

"Med bay now!" I pushed through the twins and rushed to take Val.

"What the *vaat* happened?" Evi asked as she followed, wasting no time questioning me.

"The owner had *Fellor* slave bracelets."

"*Vaat.* I didn't know those were still around."

"Me either. Val's lost a lot of blood, please tell me your system is set for humans." I set Val down gently on the metal table I had been strapped down to days earlier.

"I mean, we tried our best, but it's not like humans are common here," Avi replied as he worked on reattaching her hand. Evi worked on a tablet adjusting the several tubes that were now attached to Val. I stood back and watched, I had no expertise here and I needed to trust that the twins knew what they were doing.

I watched as the numbers on the screen turned—to what I thought were normal readings. The twins slowed their frantic pace. I felt the weight fall off my shoulders, relief spreading over me. I took a step forward, grabbing her cool hand, and placed a kiss on her knuckles.

Val was going to be okay.

It was too late for me now, I couldn't go back. I couldn't lose her, not again. For the first time ever I was glad I had failed a mission because that would keep Val closer for longer. There was a lot out on this side of the universe I was sure Val would eventually come to love. I would just have to convince her of that. And without the *Heart of the Renari* I had the time to do that.

I felt the cool metal of a blaster push against my back. I lifted my hands slowly, as J'tan spoke. "Time for your side of the deal."

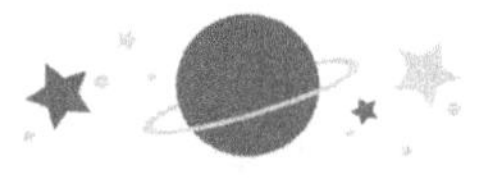

THIRTY-TWO

Star System 83

VAL

The familiar smell of musty air and metal filled my nose. Soft beeps of machines sounded around me, and I instantly knew where I was.

Back on The Revenge.

Tears pricked at my eyes as the familiar sensations caused my muscles to relax. *Safe at last.* I had never really considered the old ship my home. I had planned to leave as soon as I stepped foot on it. Now it felt more like home than ever. Opening my eyes, my view was filled with Evi and Avi peering over me.

"Told you she would wake up fast," Evi said, helping me sit up.

I looked at my left hand, surprised, yet grateful it was still there. I flexed my fingers, as tingles spread throughout my hand. My clothing caught my eye—I was back in my usual jumpsuit, the Grihan silks nowhere to be seen.

"Sara said it was lame to put it back on, but robot hands don't really feel the same. I did my best, but I'm not a doctor and some of your nerves couldn't re-connect, sorry," Avi said as he pulled the IV out of my arm.

The removal didn't even make me flinch. I felt like nothing could after that amount of pain.

"I'm just glad I still have a hand, thank you. The other women, where are they?"

"J'tan is showing them how to use blasters. They were pretty insistent on learning how to use them after watching you two," Evi replied as she helped Avi shut down the scanner.

I was grateful they made it out okay even with Jordan's betrayal. Everything in our plan had seemed to go wrong but we still made it somehow. The last week had felt years long and now I could finally take a breather.

"Is Te'ryn okay?" I stood up, feeling a little shaky, but otherwise like nothing had happened. Avi and Evi suddenly became hyper focused on the tasks of putting the rest of the machines and vials away.

"Where's Te'ryn?" I felt my heartbeat speed up. If he was hurt or worse because of me I could never forgive myself.

"Well you know, he is wanted after all…" Avi dwindled on the last word.

"Where is he?"

"In the brig, but don't get any ideas. J'tan told us to keep you away from him." Avi helped me sit back down.

My emotions took more out of me than I thought, causing my legs to sway beneath me. "Can't you guys just let it go, just this once?" I looked at both of them, their tall frames towering over me.

"Told ya she fell for him," Evi said, slapping hands with Avi, the ping of credits being passed sounding between them.

"Hey! You made a bet about that too?" I felt my cheeks burn. I stood up a little too fast causing the world to whirl. The twins attempted to help steady me, but I pushed their hands away and marched straight to the dock.

I smacked the panel to the doors. Taking out my frustration on the tech didn't help the maelstrom of emotions whirling inside me. Sure Te'ryn was wanted, and for good reason. But I couldn't justify aiding in turning him in. *Not after he saved me.* If money was the issue I had an alternative. I felt around in the intricate braids Jordan helped style and pulled out the *Heart of the Renari*. With this, I had enough to shuttle all the women and myself back to Earth, as well as help *The Revenge's* team fix the old ship. A smile crept across my face as I stepped onto the bridge.

J'tan watched with arms crossed as the two women fired at a set of holograms.

"If you're asking about the assassin, my answer is no," he said, unmoving.

"I have something to make up for his bounty."

"If it's the *Heart of the Renari*, I want nothing to do with it. That will just cause more problems than it solves. We'll return it to the Empire."

"J'tan, that's not-"

He turned to me, his gaze fierce. "You would risk everyone's lives on this ship for that, for him? He's a killer, he doesn't care about the lives of anyone. You're smarter than that, Val!"

J'tan's voice echoed throughout the dock. The women stopped firing and turned to look at us. I had only hoped they hadn't been equipped with translators yet. He continued. "He started a war for *vaats* sake. He doesn't care about the consequences as long as he gets what he wants."

"You don't know him." I stood firm, refusing to look away.

"I know his type too well. I know Alderian males too. I'm ending this before you get hurt." A pained look crossed his face before he turned back to the women.

They both awkwardly avoided my eyes and attempted to reload. I spun on my heels, anger pulsing through my veins. J'tan was right, it was already dangerous enough that we were here.

But I couldn't just sit around and let them hand over Te'ryn. I stomped through the hallways taking more of my anger out on the floor. *Helpless again.* That's all I'd ever been since I was brought out to this side of the universe. I stopped outside of the doors of the brig, not sure how to face Te'ryn.

"Is that a *massaye* out there, or is something bothering you, Val? I could hear you all the way from the dock," Te'ryn said, his words muffled by the thick metal door separating us.

"It's a *massaye*, it's crazy how they got one in here." I sighed. I had no idea what to say. I had half a mind just to leave, but I couldn't do that, not to him.

"Can you come in? I need to see for myself that you're okay."

I hit the panels and the doors slid open. Te'ryn sat in one of the three glass cells, looking as unbothered as ever. Other than the blood splatters across the black silks, he looked pristine, as if he had walked straight out of a renaissance painting.

He took one look at my face and jumped up. He pressed his hand against the glass. I returned the gesture.

"I didn't think you'd be that upset about not getting a robot arm." He smiled.

"Yeah, I really wanted a rocket launcher

hand." I forced a half smile. I didn't have the heart to tell him.

"I can get that, you know." He said softly.

"No you can't, they're turning you in." I looked away. I wasn't sure how he'd react. But Te'ryn surprised me by laughing. I looked up, startled.

"Is that what you're so sad about? Don't worry I've—we've been in worse situations, we'll get out of this one too."

I gave him a smile, of course I wasn't going to leave him here. I remembered our first meeting and the crazy past week. I had grown to like Te'ryn—a lot. "Why did you give me a translator with a tracker in it?" I asked, remembering what Ke'dan had said.

"I wanted to see you again."

"You know you could have just asked for contact information."

"A second chance encounter seemed more romantic." Te'ryn smiled and moved his hand to the door, giving it a push. It slid open easily.

"How did you do that?"

Te'ryn replied by grabbing the back of my head and pulling me into a kiss. My hands found his face and I opened my mouth, my tongue tangling with his. He lifted me with ease, gripping my ass. He pushed my back against the glass.

Te'ryn pressed a kiss against my lips. He set

me down then grabbed my hand and pulled me into the hallway. We walked quietly checking each corner till we made it to the escape pods.

"Come with me, please." His eyes softened. He looked more vulnerable than I'd ever seen him.

"You know I can't. It's just your Alderian hormones that make you so infatuated with me, you know." I opened the door to the small escape pod. While it was large enough to fit three grown Alderians, they wouldn't fit comfortably. I fumbled for the pin that held his robe together, finally releasing it, sending the silks to the ground.

"No, it's because it's you Val. Even if you were an Azzek I would still want you." Te'ryn wasted no time in removing my clothes. His hands slid up and down my body as he kissed down my neck to my chest. He took a breast in his mouth, causing me to let out a soft sigh.

"I love it when you do that." I felt Te'ryn's hot breath tickle my skin as he led me to the small sofa in the escape pod. He kissed down my stomach leaving a trail of goosebumps in his wake.

"We have to get you out of here before they notice." I gasped as his tongue found my sensitive bud.

"We have time," he said, then continued to swirl his tongue causing my muscles to tense. I pressed a hand to my mouth muffling the moan that escaped. The sensation grew and I climaxed. After he was sure I was satisfied, Te'ryn's eyes rose, meeting mine.

"Tell me you want more," Te'ryn said as he ran his thumb along his bottom lip then licked up the last of my release.

"I do," I said breathily. This was the last time I would ever see him. He was like a drug and I needed my last fix. Te'ryn kept eye contact, his silver eyes gleaming. I grabbed his cock, running my hands up and down. Te'ryn threw his head back, enjoying each stroke.

"I need you, Val."

I didn't ask in which way. This would be the last time, I would make sure of it. I gripped his length, positioning it at my entrance. He thrusted inside as another gasp escaped my lips. He stretched me further than I'd ever been, but it felt more pleasurable than painful.

He kissed me, more passionate, more desperate. "Leave with me," he said in my ear as he thrusted again.

"I can't," I moaned.

His pace picked up and we clutched each other tightly for as long as it took Te'ryn and I to climax together.

Afterwards, we took a minute to catch our breaths as we laid still in each other's arms. He pressed another kiss to my lips then helped me stand up.

"So what, you'll choose this? Making scraps and working forever just to get back to your disease-ridden primitive planet? For what? Just to do something boring like *front-algernering?* Then dying before you can even make it one-hundred cycles?" Te'ryn reached for the clothes on the ground then stood, back turned away from me.

"It's front end engineering, and yes that is exactly what I want. Believe it or not, boring is what I like. Not having to hide away in a ship all the time because I'm human, terrified I might get sold off to be some kind of entertaining pet. And even if I live only twenty more years, at least I will be free." I snatched my clothes out of Te'ryn's hands.

I fumbled with the fabric, attempting to pull my legs through, my chest heaving. A thud sounded as the *Heart of the Renari* fell out of my pocket. Te'ryn grabbed it off the floor.

"You really are good at taking things that aren't yours." He chuckled as he inspected it closer. He slid it into a hidden pocket in his silks. "If you aren't coming with me, I'm staying."

"You can't! You know what will happen if you stay. Please go." I reached for his hand, giving it a tight squeeze.

"Val, I think we both know who is the more

stubborn one between us," he replied, a cocky smirk on his face.

An idea crossed my mind.

"Okay I'll go."

A true smile stretched across Te'ryn's face at my response. I wrapped my arms around his neck, pulling him in for another kiss. I slid my hand in the hidden pocket, gently removing the *Heart of the Renari*. I didn't like doing this to Te'ryn, but I had promised the others I would get them back to Earth and this was the only way.

His hands reached up for my hair, and before they could reach their destination, I hooked my leg around the back of his knee and pulled. Using his height against him I sent him to the ground. "Thank you for everything." I jumped back out of the escape pod and slapped the button to release it.

Te'ryn jumped up and pounded his fists against the glass door separating us. "Val! Don't do this!" He shouted as he futilely messed with the controls to stop the launch.

"I'm sorry, this is the best choice, " I said.

"There's always another choice, Val."

"Not for us there isn't."

I wasn't entirely sure if I believed what I was saying. I cared about Te'ryn, but that wouldn't change the fact that we were two very different people who belonged in very different places. I had already given up half my life for one man, and I vowed I would never do that again.

"I'll find you, Val. No matter where you go, I'll find you," Te'ryn said as the pod disconnected from the ship. The engines roared to life and it shot off, disappearing into the dark black of space.

I slid to the ground, tears threatening to form. *Come on don't cry, you just met the guy.* But my heart didn't seem to get the memo.

Star System 3

VAL

"Guess this is it." I faced Avi, Evi and J'tan before boarding the massive spaceship that sat docked above the several dark oceans of Undri. I was a little disappointed that I wouldn't get the chance to see more of Avi's and Evi's home, but the ship was scheduled to leave soon.

We had managed to find passage to the star system nearby Earth's, on an Undrian exploration vessel. It was headed by several scientists in search of new life to categorize and add to their database. They were especially eager to let us join—with a large donation of course. J'tan had turned in the *Heart of the Renari*, gaining a large bounty in return. Although the bounty on Te'ryn and I still stood, I would no longer have to worry about it once I reached Earth. It would soon become a thing of the past.

Just like Te'ryn. I pushed that thought away, I

had made my choice, and while I was sure I made the right choice, I couldn't help but wonder if he was okay.

"Guess this is the end. You did alright as a bounty hunter, so if you're ever on this side of the galaxy again and looking for a job-"

"She was awful and you know it, but we'll miss you and you're always welcome back," Avi said cutting off J'tan.

I wiped a tear from my eye and smiled. It was strange how these aliens felt like family after just one year, when I had never felt that way with the family I'd known my entire life.

"Give those humans hell, Val." Evi smirked.

I pulled the three large aliens in for one last hug, a human custom that they tolerated on my behalf.

"You know I will. Thank you. Truly." I gave them one last wave and walked up the wide ramp that led to the belly of the ship.

I wiped another tear from my cheek, then took in a breath to steady myself. *I'm finally going home.*

One month later

I exited my small room, furnished only with a bed, and several lockers hidden behind panels in the wall. It was tight but it was only temporary. Not to mention the ride back had been incredibly more comfortable than the ride here. Time flew by and we had finally reached our destination—we were close to Earth. I gave my room one last look, pulling the small bag of my belongings over my shoulder. I walked slowly through the dimly lit halls, nearly running into a scientist. I muttered an apology and continued on my way. Undrians didn't need as much light to see so this had become a common occurrence in my time here. I missed the light, but I didn't care as much since I would be getting plenty soon. I continued my path to the dock, where the other women were waiting.

I was greeted by the captain and several other scientists as I entered. "We wish you the best on your journey home," the captain said, giving the typical Undrian bow.

"And we'll make sure to name a new species we find in honor of your contribution," a scientist with a high pitched voice piped in.

"Name it Godzilla," Sara said.

Lynn and I chuckled at the inside joke. The scientist looked perplexed at the joke, but kept the smile on her face.

"We will name any new species *Godzilla,* then."

We all said our final goodbyes, and the crew looked sad to see us go. They had been fascinated with the various types of life on Earth. We'd given them information they legally would not have been able to gain otherwise. It was not often that Undrians, or any of the alien races, would get the chance to learn about the mysterious humans and the world they lived on. The quirky scientists with their unending questions had grown on us all, but we were ready to finally go home.

We filed in onto the small cruiser we had purchased to finish the final leg of our trip. J'tan had argued with me that it was important to find the perfect ship, and made us wait a couple more weeks before he could obtain one that was up to his standards. He had used the rest of the money gained from the bounty to buy it. Grumpy as he pretended to be, he really did care. I would miss him and the others greatly but I was going back to where I belonged.

Right?

I took the helm and sent the small ship towards our destination, putting all my memories of my space adventure behind me.

Our excitement stayed strong even as we spent the next three days traveling. Everyone seemed to have complicated emotions about returning home. Fear and excitement being the main two. As we passed Jupiter, the other two joined me near the helm, eagerly watching the familiar planets fly by.

"How do you think we're going to explain our absence for a year and a half?" Lynn asked.

"I'm sure we'll figure something out," I replied.

"Let's just go on some documentary and say we got abducted by aliens, then get rich," Sara said, nudging Lynn.

We all laughed at the suggestion but stopped abruptly as a blue planet came into view.

Earth.

We had finally made it home.

Epilogue

TE'RYN

The familiar stink of silversalt, sweaty bodies and booze hit me as I entered Club Eclipse. Busier than ever, I ignored the masses as I set my sights on the yellow tinted box that overlooked the dance floor. I stalked my way down to the crowds of dancing bodies, forcing my way through.

"Move," I growled, pushing a male out of the way.

I walked up the flashing stairs, only coming to a stop when a Basillian guard blocked my path.

"Name," the guard croaked.

"Not important." I struck its neck with my black dagger, sending the Basillian down the stairs, its body landing at the bottom with a sickening crack.

The second guard lunged at me, but its large

size slowed it down. I was able to take the guard down with my other dagger before it could even reach me. Not missing a beat, I stepped over the fallen guard and continued on my path. I pushed the doors to the Basillian's room open. The doors banged against the walls from the force.

The Basillian informant—the one who had left me for dead on that planet, sat in the room, drink in hand. Its head swung up at my entrance, eyes filling with fear as soon as it recognized my face.

"You really have some guts to pull something like that on me," I said as I stepped forward.

The Basillian jumped up, its hand reaching for the blaster on the table. I swung a dagger at the Basillian. It let out a yowl as the dagger pinned its hand to the table.

"Surely we can come to a compromise," the Basillian said, its voice high pitched and rambling.

I kicked it in the stomach, forcing it to its knees. I squatted to the Basillian's level, meeting its eyes. "I'm sure we can." I gave its back a pat.

I sat on the opposing chair, grabbing a glass of the Aged Greco. "I need credits, a lot of them." I swirled the amber liquor and downed it in one gulp.

"I'll give you as many as you want, just don't

kill me," the Basillian said, large beads of sweat trickling down its textured skin.

"Six-hundred-thousand."

"But thats-"

"Your life is worth less than that?" I raised an eyebrow as I fiddled with the black dagger in my hand.

"No, release me and I'll give them to you."

I pulled the dagger free from the Basillian's flesh and it let out a hiss of pain. It pulled a swatch of cloth from its breast pocket, wrapping it around the bleeding wound and quickly got to work on its palmpad, setting up the credits for transfer. I held out my palm, meeting it with the Basillian's, causing a ping to sound, ensuring the credits were transferred. I verified the amount then made my way to the door.

"Oh, and you forgot, I'm an assassin, not a *vaating* pacifist." I spun, sending a dagger flying.

It hit the Basillian square in the eyes. Its body slumped in the chair.

Dead.

I left the room leaving the body behind. Now that I had my revenge, and my credits, there was nothing stopping me from finding Val.

And find her I will.

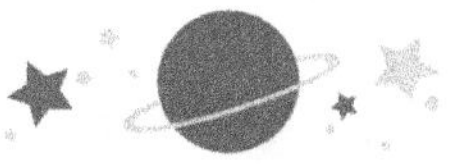

Author Bio

Lauren Winther has always dreamed of being pulled into another world. While waiting for her valiant quest to come, she writes stories about characters being pulled into extraordinary situations.

laurenwinther.com

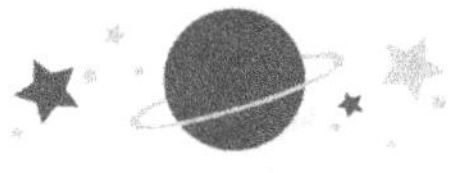

A Sneak Peek of Book Two

A GALAXY OF DEBTS

Star System 30003 (AKA, Earth's Star System)

"Vaat, another dead end." I cursed, watching the scanner impatiently as it searched the small blue planet beneath me. Val's planet was more advanced than I had thought—making it almost impossible to find just one human. I pulled up another screen on my ship's dashboard looking through the human's social database that included a long list of people named Val. It was dismaying how many were listed on it. I'd spent a fortune to get here but my knowledge of her was severely limited.

"Come on." I pleaded with the scanner, hoping it would pick up on any non-human technology I was sure Val would have on her.

Nothing.

I groaned as I stood from the pilot's seat. The technology on this new ship was better, but I couldn't help but miss my old one. This one still smelled new and normally, I would be delighted at that, but it was missing the memories of the small human I was desperately searching for.

For now.

I returned to my bedroom, this one furnished with a large bed and my favorite set of silky sheets from Aldar—finally laying down to rest after several hours of focus. I activated my palmpad searching through the human's cataloged videos. The simple-looking letters were translated quickly to ones I could understand as I scrolled through the categories. Various videos of humans cooking, re-enacted tales, and discussions of politics populated the screen. I'd spent the last several rotations learning more about the planet Val called home. A video titled *"Moon landing faked"* scrolled into view. Amused, I clicked.

As the video played I chuckled. *Which race would lie about space travel?* I spent the next several hours watching suggested videos one after another. Each entailing the many secrets that had been kept from the population. I didn't know why Val wanted to live on a planet where governments would lie about landing on the moon. *She's lucky I'm coming after her.* Entranced by the mysteries of her world I continued watching till I fell asleep.

I was startled awake by loud music as my holo remained on, still playing the human videos. I squinted, blinded by the light as a holo featuring an older human male—with dark skin and a receding hairline—came into view. Moving to turn it off, I was stopped by a familiar tale.

"So anyways, my daughter was taken to this planet called Greenan."

"It's Grihan, Dad," a familiar voice corrected the male from off-screen.

"Right. And then her friend rescued her and brought her home, what was your friend's name again?"

"Val."

"Right. Val."

I paused the video.

I calibrated the holo and scanned the data of the video looking for any information about where it had been filmed. *Finally, I've found my first lead.* My holo pinged as it pulled up the coordinates—somewhere in the middle of a place called Illinois. I dashed to the bridge—cursing at how much longer it took to get there with the larger size of my new ship. I set the new coordinates, wasting no time to depart.

I was anxious the whole trip down into Earth's atmosphere. From what I knew, the humans didn't have the technology needed to detect my ship. But the human's government liked to keep secrets about moon landings and several other things as well, so I kept an eye on the scanners around me as I descended, watching for any incoming projectiles.

I let out a sigh of relief as I hovered over a small field illuminated by the small singular moon hanging in the sky. I'd made it down safely. I landed in the middle of a flattened circle surrounded by tall plants with a yellow bulbous shape at the top. I kept the stealth on my ship, not exactly sure what to expect from the human called Mr. King—I could only hope that he didn't have his house armed.

I exited my ship and pushed my way through the long green stalks. I approached the small house built out of organic matter. *Why would humans make a home out of something so weak? It could blow away or even rot.* I stopped in my tracks as I heard shuffling nearby. I tapped my holo ring around my neck, shifting my image into that of a human male. I held my dagger, prepared for the attacker. Creeping low to the ground, I snuck towards the sound. Ready to strike first.

In the clearing stood a large animal with four legs and horns, unbothered by my appearance as it continued grazing on the grass around it. I pulled my hand out, checking my holo for information on the animal. It was called a cow, and was relatively harmless. I relaxed my muscles and returned my dagger to its sheath. I was getting jumpy for no reason. No way a cow or a human would be a threat to me.

Click-click.

I spun towards the sound and found the man I was looking for—Mr. King—holding a double-barreled blaster—*wait, gun*—in my direction.

"Don't move," he commanded.

I kept silent. *How can I get him to talk?*

"What are you doing here?"

Maybe I could torture him for the info?

"I said, what are you doing here?" He held his gun higher for emphasis.

No, Val wouldn't like that.

"The horsepower in my truck stopped running…" I recalled one of the several advertisements bombarding the videos I watched. I held my unarmed hands out in a gesture of peace.

"It's awfully late to be driving."

"Yeah, it's very late. I'm just uh, trying to get home."

He held my gaze for a while, uncertainty still in his eyes. I tried to remember my knowledge of the human's culture and then asked, "can I use your cellular telephone?"

Taken aback he stumbled over his words. "Uh, what…sure, I guess."

Taking the opportunity, I started towards his home. He followed behind me, muttering something about "kids and their phones." I pulled open the frail door, nearly removing it from its hinges. I muttered an apology and ducked through the low doorway. I needed to remember that Alderians were much stronger than humans. His living space was small. It contained a small table with four chairs, a sink and other machines I didn't know the name of.

"You can sit here. The phone's charging, I'll go get it."

"Thank you." I gave him a smile to help ease the tension but he glared as he walked up the stairs.

The sound of creaking followed him up the stairs and I wandered around the home, looking at the decor. In one room I found plush seating and an ancient-looking screen. Hanging on the wall next to it was a picture of Mr. King and the small human Sara, standing next to each other with smiles on their faces.

"Is this your daughter?" I asked as he walked into the room behind me.

"Yeah and here's the phone, call your ride and get out of here."

I took the small phone from his hand, unable to read the characters and shapes that filled the screen. I couldn't risk startling the human by using my palmpad. I handed him back the phone.

"Call Sara."

"Wait, who are you?" The male asked as he stepped back.

"Call her while I'm asking nicely, I'm looking for her friend."

He didn't listen and ran towards the gun in the other room. I sighed as I flung a dagger in his direction, grazing his face. It lodged in the tall metal box in front of him and he froze at the impact.

"You're one of *them*."

"Yeah yeah, call her now." I was behind him before he could react, holding my dagger at his throat.

He swallowed and pushed several buttons on the phone. I could hear the sound of ringing coming through the device. He put the phone up to his ear, still watching me nervously.

"Sara. There's-"

I plucked the phone from his hand and positioned it against my own ear. "Sara, where's Val? She owes me."

"What- you better not have done anything to my dad," Sara yelled over the device, forcing me to yank it away to save my hearing.

"If you want him safe, then tell me where she is." I held my palmpad up to the ancient device, pulling up Sara's location as well as her message feed. If she messaged Val now, I would be able to track it to her.

"I'm not telling you anything, get over her. She broke up with you."

I had become distracted in my conversation

with Sara. By the time I looked up, King had retrieved his gun, pointing it in my direction.

"Oh, you really don't want to do that," I said, dropping the phone. I took a step towards the small human as he fired a shot in my direction.

www.ingramcontent.com/pod-product-compliance
Lightning Source LLC
Chambersburg PA
CBHW071457140726
47997CB00005B/1764